Kaz Cooke is a cartoonist a̶... include *Real Gorgeous*, the *... Yourself Nice*. She lives i̶... maintains an unseemly int̶... and nurses a pathological ... executives and of people ..... crystals in their pockets. But that's Sagittarians for you.

The Crocodile Club is her first novel.

THE CROCODILE CLUB

KAZ COOKE

Allen & Unwin

This story is fiction. It bears no relation to real people or events. Some Darwin locations and institutions are referred to, but they are not to be taken literally. My Darwin friends will know the Territory is not yet a State and that there are no Indonesian fishing expeditions or public military excercises on the eve of the Wet Season. I hope they will forgive such factual travesties in the name of art, or possibly slovenliness.

Information about the struggle for land justice by Aboriginal people in the Northern Territory is available from the Northern Land Council, Stuart Highway, Darwin, and the Central Land Council, Stuart Highway, Alice Springs.

This paperback edition, 1997
First published in 1992 by
Allen & Unwin
9 Atchison Street
St Leonards NSW 2065
Australia
Phone: (61 2) 9901 4088
Fax: (61 2) 9906 2218
E-mail: frontdesk@allen-unwin.com.au
URL:http://www.allen-unwin.com.au

National Library of Australia
Cataloguing-in-Publication entry:

Cooke, Kaz, 1962– .
The crocodile club.
ISBN 1 86448 315 6.
I. Title.

A823.3

Set in Palatino by Midland Typesetters, Maryborough, Victoria
Printed by Australian Print Group, Maryborough, Victoria

Designed by Redback Graphix, Annandale, Sydney

The lyrics from the Mental As Anything song 'Live It Up' were written by Greedy Smith and used by kind permission of Syray Music.

10 9 8 7 6 5

Contents

Acknowledgements

Several people need a damned good thanking. The Queen of Quirk, Ms Shrewdness herself, Jennifer Saunders; most verily the all-abseiling original Boopsie and darling of the wimple set, that old Gail Davidson; Trudy Hayter, who downed tools and fled her shed many times to lighten my load; Mr John Clarke, Baronet of Thong, whose encouragement and first aid was only rivalled by the spookily talented Philippa Hawker's; Douglas 'Snake-Hips' Tremlett, who tore himself from the dance floor to provide advice on magic, and possibly whisky (but who can remember?); my agent 'Six Gun' Dennehy; the radio maven with street cred, Helen Thomas; lollapalooza lenswoman Ponchita Hawkes; The Princess of All Ireland and Brunswick Street, Kathleen McCann; my publisher, Miss Jewels; and of course the Darwin mob, led by Chips Mackinolty and including Lulubella Inglis, Wild Thing Elderton, Marie McMahon, Lady Jenny Blokland, Lord James Throgmorton Gallacher, Sandra Fong and Danny Markovich, the Cookes, Prince Malcolm Ormiston and the mellifluous phantom. And thank you to the groovestar of design heaven, art wrangler Michael Callaghan. And Mum, Dad, John, Em, and Glenda for family stuff.

Any errors of judgement in this story are to be blamed collectively and entirely on those people mentioned here. It pains me that none of them can explain why I woke up in the middle of the night and wrote the following in my novel notebook: 'Lap-top sulking, Burl Ives, Irish folk-dance, Russian Kombi van or dog's breakfast?'.

You be the judge.

Kaz Cooke, Melbourne, 1991

vii

Pre-Menstrual As Anything

Darwin, December 1997

It was a dank and steamy night.

That's how it is during the Build-up—long, oppressive days and sweat-logged nights, for weeks and weeks before the Big Wet. Even the darkness doesn't bring relief. Ninety-seven per cent humidity. Ninety-nine per cent insanity.

Out past the yachts and certainly past the drinkers at the Darwin Yacht Club Bar, who rarely bothered to look up, the sun had slipped suddenly under the horizon. Locals were standing in their pools, or settling into another stubby of beer on the verandah, or flaked out under ceiling fans switched to helicopter frenzy. Others turned their bedrooms into chilly bunkers; air-conned cool-stores with condensation dripping down the wall. Inside it was dank, outside it was still and steamy.

The beach was quiet. The tourists had gone, and the hippies and Swedish-looking Rastafarians in their creaky Kombi vans wouldn't come back until the next Dry Season. In the water a few cruising crocodiles nudged deadly jellyfish. The locals knew better than to attempt a midnight swim.

Up near the line of mangroves, two human crocodiles were pretending that the sandflies hadn't found a way into their trousers. One man was wearing a light-weight, beige suit, the other was a shorts-and-long-socks man, and they both made an effort not to scratch. The two stood uneasily in the sand and shook hands. In the dark, neither could see the other's eyes very clearly.

The taller man in the beige suit put his hands on his hips and shifted his weight to make his beer gut the centre of gravity. Looking across the bay at the squat pyramid of the Darwin casino building, he grinned.

'Bigger than that one, mate,' he said softly.

The other man nodded. 'And nobody will know until we get the bloody foundations in,' he said. 'Right?'

'No worries.'

The Great Salami was taking off his make-up. 'Boopsie,' he said, 'We must speak.' The light bulbs surrounding the mouldy mirror had blown long ago, and he had to lean over the bench and squint to get the last bits around his eyes. He took off his turban, wrapped his baby-pink chenille dressing-gown around him, fiddled with one end of a magic wand, and sighed.

Selina Plankton, known to The Great Salami, her boss, as Boopsie, shimmied out of a spangly silver tutu and picked up her jeans. 'Don't tell me, the rabbit's got the runs again. Look, it's not my fault. I forgot to feed it. It's just contrary.'

The Great Salami looked around the dressing-room. The twenty-five-watt globe barely made an impact on the heaps of lurex costumes, old take-away containers and pieces of magic paraphernalia. A sign in blue Biro on a torn bit of paper was stuck to the damp wall: 'Turn the light Off when you Leave. It save's mony the Managment.'

Piled on the floor were big metal trick rings; scarves; metal bottles; plastic flowers; Porkie and Beth, the doves, in their orange milk crate with chicken wire on the top; and Keating, the white rabbit, sulking in his hutch. Keating had been known to bite schoolchildren and poop on distinguished members of the audience during his reckless bids for freedom.

Selina was talking through her favourite, old, black jumper as she struggled to pull it over a tangle of red hair that was often brown, and sometimes

3

yellow, and sometimes all three at once. 'I swear to you, Keith, if that moth-eaten rabbit wees on me one more time I'm going to take him up the farm and get Mum to do a Sunday casserole.' Her head popped through the top of the jumper and she pulled it sharply down over her hips, stretching the wool to its limits.

'I mean it. Where did I put my socks? God, is it really midnight? Keating gave that woman in the front row a real spray in the second half tonight. How did they get there? She'll never get it off those suede high-heels. They probably cost more than a month's pay for both of us.' She looked up at the Great Salami, pushing her hair off her face. It was a kind face, with generous features, light brown eyes with crinkly laugh lines underneath them and a big smile that went kind of sideways, except when she grinned.

Selina drew herself up to her full height of five feet four inches. 'Keith,' she said sternly. 'You look bloody awful. Come on, I'll buy you a coffee at Cantina and take you home.' It was the least she could do for the magician and hypnotist who had rescued her from wool-classing and put her on the dilapidated stage of the Collingwood Zippo Club (no shorts, no thongs, no refunds) in Smith Street. It didn't pay well, but it was show biz, and she didn't have to deal with dumb animals, except Keating.

The Great Salami (alias Keith Tremble) had been good to her. He didn't try to feel her up, apologised when she had to do something shitty, and made her coffee more often than he asked for one. He

4

was funny, too. On their first night at the Zippo, after they'd rehearsed for weeks and she'd solemnly sworn the Magicians' Secret Oath, he'd handed her a matchbox in the dressing-room before the show.

'Here's your costume, Boopsie,' he'd said. 'You'll find a spare in there too, just in case.'

Now, over a year later, she knew that she was working with a magician who cared more about his work than dressing his assistant like a stripper. He'd had her going there for a minute, though. She had been about to let fly when something made her shake the box. It was full of matches.

He protected her on stage, too; taught her how to handle it when the buck's nights got too rowdy, when a table full of hoons called for the twelfth jug from long-suffering waitresses. When somebody got out of hand and yelled 'Sit on my face!', she had a million lines ready, although one night Keith had hit on the best one: 'Sir! What you ask eez eempossible! My bee-yood-iful assistant Boopsie has been instructed by me, ze Great Salami . . . never to sit on anything uglier zan her own arsehole!' The pensioners had loved it.

'I'm rooted,' he was saying, 'And I've got some bad news.'

'Oh, hell,' said Selina, flinging herself into a purple vinyl armchair with one missing leg, and pulling on her black ripple-soled desert boots; she didn't bother to untie the laces. It was a small struggle. 'Come on, kabana-face, out with it. Did management give you a hard time about the lady's shoes? I saw O'Toole giving you the rounds of

5

the men's room. They should get the doors fixed.'

The Great Salami looked at Selina and tears filled his eyes. 'We got fired, Boops.'

'Oh, no. Oh, Keith.' Selina reached out and held his hand. 'But you've had the Saturday night gig for three years! They can't do this to you! Was it Keating? Those bastards! Just one little wee and you're out on your ear! I can't believe it!' She was crying too.

'It's progress, Boopsie. Wet T-shirts. Cocktails with dirty names. They want a disc jockey who'll swear. Nobody wants people any more. They'll play Rod Stewart.' Selina stopped crying at once. 'They will,' Keith insisted. 'They're going to paint the place pink and grey. Punters who won't sit on a shandy for an hour and a half. Try to break the Last Laugh's hold on the market down here.'

'Come on, matey,' said Selina, 'let's pack up this stuff and go home. Maybe it won't seem so bad in the morning.'

'Leave it, Boops. We've got one more show to do. Next Saturday. And we'll go out in style. Howdja like to be sawn in half, kid?'

'I'd rather saw O'Toole in half and send him to the dog-food factory,' said Selina.

'What have you got against those poor puppy dogs?' smiled The Great Salami. 'Let's go and get pissed.'

They left the light on.

Arriving home at 3 am, feeling only slightly shickered, and skipping up the last two stairs, Selina found an official-looking notice with the real-estate agent's letterhead on it, nailed to the front door of her flat. 'That's a bit much,' she said to herself. 'What's wrong with the letter-box, you wankers?'

Selina let herself in, hit the light, threw her bag of stage costumes on the bed and flung herself after it, still holding the notice. She uncrumpled it, angled its face towards the light, and read . . .

LANDLORD'S NOTICE TO TENANT TO VACATE ON SPECIFIED GROUNDS FORM 29 SECTION 122
Tenant: Selina Plankton, 2/678 Groad Street, Collingwood
Owner: Sprauncey Investments, PO Box 9087B92-2 St Kilda, Victoria
Tenant to vacate on Saturday 12 December at 10.30 am.
File Number 768
Reason for notice (please tick)
A) To be demolished
B) To be substantially repaired, renovated, or reconstructed where said repair, renovation or reconstruction cannot be carried out practicably without vacant possession
C) To be used for the purposes of business or for any other purpose not being a purpose of letting as a residence
D) To be occupied:
   i) By the landlord, his spouse, child, parent or spouse's parent, or
   ii) By another person who normally lives with the

7

landlord and is wholly or substantially dependent on him

E) To be sold or offered for sale with vacant possession

F) Being the property of a public statutory authority which is authorised to acquire compulsorily land for its purposes—required for public purposes.

It was signed and dated 5 December and there was a dirty big tick next to option A.

Selina looked at the ceiling; she'd had enough for one day. 'You complete mongrels,' she said quietly, then folded up the notice into a paper plane, opened the front door, and launched it on the still night air. 'So arrest me for littering!' she shouted, and tiptoed back inside, closing the door quietly behind her.

She had changed into her jarmies and snuggled up in bed. 'Just think,' she said to herself before she fell asleep, 'next week I'm going to be thrown on to the streets and sawn in half in one day. That's something to look forward to, isn't it?'

Manangatang, North-western Victoria, Sunday 6 December, 8 am

The verandah door squeaked and slammed. 'Muuuuuuu-um,' shouted Selina's dad. 'Our girl's on the phone!'

Selina's mum was gathering eggs in the chookhouse and putting them carefully in her apron pockets. She fastened the door firmly behind her and shouted back, 'Tell her I'm on me way, Len.' She strolled to the other side of the yard, picked an aphid off the rose bushes, inspected it closely and squished it, then leaned down and let the border collie off her chain. On the verandah she changed her gumboots for blue house slippers, then wiped them on the mat.

Dot took the eggs out of her pockets and put them in the wire basket on the kitchen bench. She washed her hands at the sink, dried them on a tea-towel which she hung neatly on the front of the stove, and walked into the hallway.

She heard the wire door squeak and slam again, and Len's voice from the verandah: 'I'll be down the lucerne paddock if you need us, Mum. If you go down the dunny, take the rifle. That tiger's around again . . . ' and she waited for the sound of the tractor. Then she sat down on the telephone stool, took her knitting from the shelf under the telephone book and picked up the receiver, nestling it between shoulder and chin.

'Hello, lovey,' she said.

'Mum, this is STD for God's sake.'

'Now, Sellie, you're getting too impatient down there. It's Sunday, and I thought you'd rigged up the phone box with your hairpin?'

'Yes, Mum, but they fixed it. It hasn't been a good week. I'm getting evicted.'

'What have you done?'

'Nothing! They're going to tear down the building. And I got the sack because they've sacked Keith.'

'What's he done?'

'Mu-um! Nothing. He says they just want to tart the place up and put in DJs in wet T-shirts. I don't know what to do.'

Dot clucked over the soft sounds of her needles working. 'Well, lovey, you know you can always come home. Um . . . there's a snake in the dunny again and Deirdre Ruth has got morning sickness something shocking. I'm doing a cream matinee jacket for her. We'd be glad to have you, of course.'

'Thanks, Mum, but I'll try and work something out. Dad said the wool price is down again.'

'Don't you worry about us, dear. There's always room for you. And you could help your father. There's something wrong with the tractor again, and he can't find the problem. Now take care of yourself, poss, and let us know what you've decided, all right? There were only six eggs this morning, I think your Hetty's still a bit off.'

'Yeah, well don't eat her, Mum, you promised. You put it in writing, in your last letter.'

'So I did. Bye-bye, love.'

'See you, Mum. Thanks.'

'Oh, before I forget, Sellie, have you got enough money?'

'I got $125 in advance salary from the Zippo for Saturday night—Keith's going to saw me in half— but I have to pay the gas bill this week. Don't worry, I'll work something out.'

'Your dad says keep it out of Rothwell's.'

Selina rolled her eyes. 'He's been saying that since 1989.'

'Are you still seeing that what's-his-name?'

'Yes, Mum, but not for much longer, I think . . . '
'Good. He's a dickhead. Bye-bye, love.'
'See ya, Mum.'

Melbourne, Friday 11 December, 9 am

Selina put her head on the cool laminex of the kitchen table beside the employment pages. Nothing in them for her this morning, either. Just like Monday, and Tuesday, and Wednesday, and Thursday. Maybe tomorrow, although she'd be busy all day with The Great Salami rehearsing their new act, and she'd have to move her stuff out of the flat. Selina wondered if the 'demolishing' also referred to the alleged 'furnishings and appointments'.

Everything she owned would fit into her three enormous hexagonal hat-boxes, but she wasn't sure where she would take them after work on Saturday night. She was wearing her red shoes to cheer herself up, but it didn't help much. Usually Selina was the personification of *joie de vivre*. Oh, she got depressed all right, particularly when she was pre-menstrual, but that only reinforced her generally irrepressible nature. She either intoxicated or irritated people around her; consequently, the world seemed full of lunatics and cynics.

Selina crossed over to the fridge. She looked in at the same things which had confronted her fifteen minutes ago: one dead bunch of spinach (iron) some solidified milk (bones), and a carrot which looked like a water-diviner (vitamin D).

She closed the fridge door again and sat down at the table. Perhaps she could stay with her friend Kylie—'Ky' Nguyen was a Vietnamese orphan who had been adopted by Dot's bridesmaid, Shirl, and her husband Tiny—but Ky had just moved into a boarding house in Richmond run by old friends from Manangatang, Rita and Joe. They would take her in except they didn't have a vacancy and they were hardly the type to throw people on the street. During the seventies, Manangatang had gone multicultural in the same week Ky arrived, when Joseph Mgambl was appointed head teacher at Manangatang State School in a blaze of publicity. All the big city papers had come up to do stories on the racism of a country town. It may well have happened, but the townspeople closed ranks against the journalists when they discovered that Joseph could play Australian Rules Football like Rudolph Nureyev could dance. And Rudolph Nureyev would have had a hard time in Manangatang unless he was useful on the half-forward flank. Joe Mgambl may have refused to join the National Party, but he was a decent sort of utility in the goal department.

Where else? Life on the farm wasn't exactly exciting, and her other best friend, Miranda Spurn, had been sent to the Darwin office of ABC radio after throwing a devil-on-horseback at the managing director during the launch of a book she didn't agree with. The managing director hadn't minded at all; it was the most interesting thing that had happened to him all week, and he found it strangely thrilling. But Miranda's chief of staff had been looking for an excuse to transfer her because she was smarter than he was. And that was that.

Selina wondered how long she would have to wait to get a dole cheque. She'd have to go home to the farm for a while and speak to Hetty about doing her bit during a recession. The telephone rang. Selina looked at it for a while, and then picked it up.

'Hi, darling,' it said.

'Who is this?' she replied, quite sensibly under the circumstances.

'What do you mean, who is it? It's me.'

'Hello, Briian,' Selina said wearily.

'How are ya, babe? I've been flat out all week working on the plans for the low-level public housing job, and I've only just had a chance to call.'

Briian the Crazed Architect. What Selina didn't know was that Briian was once Brian, and had changed the spelling of his name to make his business card more striking. She also didn't know that Briian had never worked on an affordable housing project in his life, and that he cared more about his mobile telephone than almost anybody else, except himself. Briian pretended he worked on worthy projects because, as he explained to his mates, 'It gets you a better class of root'. He was living proof that one should never go to bed on the first date. Of course, Briian was living proof that one should never go to bed until at least the seven hundred and fifty-third date (but I digress). Selina had been out with Briian three times, and was beginning to suspect that he was a weasel.

'Briian, I'm very pleased for you, but to answer your question . . . '

'What question?'

Selina carried the phone to an armchair and flopped into it sideways, her legs dangling over the arm. 'How am I? I'm pre-menstrual and I want to burst into tears and I got the sack and tomorrow I'm being evicted. And Kylie says she saw you at Cantina on Wednesday night tongue-kissing a woman.'

'Oh, no,' said Briian, 'You can't come and stay here.'

'I don't want to stay at your place, Briian, I'm just depressed about it all. Who was the woman?'

Briian thought fast. 'She's not a woman, she's the head of development at Mega Concrete Hype Inc., and it was business. Kylie's been eating too much MSG in her flied lice! Ha, ha, ha. Well, babe, I've been really busy, but maybe you could come over tomorrow night, make us something to eat and then, you know, you could stay. Just for the night. Maybe we could have a good time, if you know what I mean.'

Selina looked quizzically at the telephone. Was the whole world populated by aliens? Had she really considered having sex with such a jerk? Could she demand a time-rewind and take it all back? Why was her mother always right? Could she possibly salvage some dignity out of this situation? Why, yes, of course she could.

14

'Briian, for God's sake, Kylie's not Chinese. And you're a racist prick. And who said you could call me babe . . . '

'Sorry, babe, there's another call.' Briian put her on hold.

Selina held. One minute. She examined the green tree frogs printed on her orange frock. Two minutes. She walked over and opened the fridge. The spinach looked a bit worse. Briian's voice interrupted 'Greensleeves'.

'Great job coming up. Could be my big break. What were you saying?'

'You're dropped, weasel-dick,' said Selina before she hung up. 'And I untuned your stereo with a hairpin because you played Billy Joel,' she said to the phone.

It rang. She picked it up.

'I never worked for public housing in my life,' said Briian.

Selina slammed the receiver down and burst into tears which brought on a cramp in her stomach. According to the calendar on the fridge, she was due tomorrow. 'I suppose if you're going to get your period, it's a good time to get sawn in half. Amazing I never thought of it before,' she mused. The thought cheered her up enough to discard the idea of going back to bed with a hot-water bottle. 'Oh, well,' she thought, 'I'll have to go out foraging, I suppose.' She put her dirty clothes in one of her hat-boxes, figuring it would be her last chance to get to the laundromat before being evicted, and checked the fridge before she left.

Selina jumped the tram down Brunswick Street

15

to the funny little milk bar—a place which seemed to be licensed to take your gas bill money and charge seven cents more than anybody else for Twisties. After paying her gas bill, Selina calculated that there was $72.16 between her and skintsville. She burst into tears again. The milk bar man ordered her out of the shop, but gave her a Choo Choo bar by way of apology.

Selina, while not one to scorn a gift Choo Choo bar, felt that her mother would have something to say about its nutritional aspect, *vis à vis* breakfast. So she put on her dark glasses, smoothed down her frock, jooshed her hair up a bit, and strode into Cantina, swinging the hat-box in a manner she wrongly assumed looked jaunty.

She had arrived in the middle of the Brunswick Street breakfast rush: at 10.30 am. The pale night-clubbers were tucking into their smoked salmon and brioche with scrambled eggs, while those over thirty were ordering the hangover special (toast, two Panadol and a cola) in tiny voices. And the Bad Cop waiters were on.

Most coffee shops hired Bad Cop waiters at peak times. Their job was to slam food down on the table, disappear when customers wanted a second coffee, and sneer. This ensured a high turnover and more money for the owners, plus a lot of patrons who wondered if they had rat's breath or had once murdered the waiter's relatives and it had slipped their minds. Selina was served immediately by a vampire who shrieked, 'One scrambled eggs and bacon for table three who doesn't care about her figure and expects me to

16

walk around her stupid suitcase and a fresh orange juice hold the pith!'

Later, as the vampire was menacing another table, Selina said, 'I just thought I should tell you that your skirt is tucked into the waistband of your pantihose at the back, lovey,' an impression of her mother which sent the vampire dashing into the kitchen and returning a moment later, rather flushed, to slam Selina's breakfast down so hard that the salt shaker fell on the floor.

'Enjoy,' she snarled.

Reflecting, Selina realised it would be much more sensible to have breakfast at 2 pm. That way, the Good Cop waiter shift encouraged you to sit a wee bit longer, have another piece of toast and chat about the form guide. Her thoughts were interrupted by a keyboard player from an obscure grunge-schmaltz band. He pressed a flyer into her hand and told her in a very tiny voice he was going to order toast and paracetamol.

'I'd love to stay and moan,' she said, 'But I must dash. Even if you go stark staring mad after I leave, don't tip that woman. We've never met before, but I feel our commitment will stretch to that. Are you with me?'

'Tell you what,' said the keyboard player. 'I'll call her babe.'

'Oooh, you rock and roll types play dirty pool,' Selina said, with her best smile, leaving the keyboard player feeling better already, but not really cheering herself. As she left, she thought about Briian the Crazed (Waste of Time) Architect and started crying again. 'Having a weep, are we, darling?' asked the vampire maliciously as she held the door open to allow a cold draught in.

Selina gave her a look, the same look that once caused a man who had yelled 'Hey, Blondie!' at her to drive half-way up the Manangatang cenotaph.

Now what? She could gaze in the bookshop window a few doors down, but that would be depressing; she now had exactly $60.17 left and didn't think it would be entirely wise to blow it on Mills and Boon novels, even if she could pretend it was research for her own unfinished romance novel, *Hornrims of Desire*. She was already well past the bookshop anyway, and there was the laundromat. It was called 'Sud Off'. A new sign in the window caught her attention: 'Psychiatrist. Upstairs. $60 an hour'.

'Good Lord,' thought Selina, because sometimes even in her thoughts she did impressions of her mother. 'What will they think of next?' She went inside, shaking her head, not so much from bemusement, but to loosen a hairpin so she could rig the soap-powder dispenser and the washing machine, in that order. Selina, as well as being a dab hand at disappearing, making objects move through tables and secreting doves about her person without spoiling the line of her frock, could use a hairpin to render almost any machine inoperable or useful in a way that had not been intended by its manufacturer.

Vera, the old woman who ran the laundromat, didn't mind because Selina had fixed up her little telly so it got SBS. They agreed there was something infinitely more satisfying about a sub-titled soap opera. But Vera was out, probably down in the front bar of the Pedestrian having a heart-starter, and the only other thing to do was read a 1974 copy of *New Idea*. Above the slooshing sounds of Washing Machine Sixteen (her favourite) Selina heard a Mental As Anything song. She hummed a little bit, 'Hey there, you with the sad face/Come up to my place/And live it up . . . ' She wondered if it was the psychiatrist. Selina skipped on to the street and looked up. The music was louder.

A head popped out of the first-floor window. The head was wearing hornrimmed glasses. It looked at her, and said, 'Hurry up, I haven't got all day,' and disappeared again.

2

Boopsie Goes to Smuggler's Cove

Selina stared at the window but the head failed to reappear. A voice behind her said, 'Mad as a cut snake, but harmless as a rabbit.'

'Hello Vera,' said Selina, without turning around. 'You don't know much about rabbits. How's the telly?'

'Beaut. What does he want to see you for?'

'I don't know. Is it safe?'

'Safe enough. He's a trick cyclist who's been helping Smuggler. Remember Smuggler, the old derro from Rae Street Park? The one who thought he was Mikhail Gorbachev when the Berlin Wall came down? The boys at the Pedestrian reckon he's all right, so I let him move in last week. Loud, but. You got a load on?'

'Yeah, Sixteen.'

'I'll look after it for you. Go up and see what he wants. If he's just skylarking, see if he wants a cuppa. I'm going to put the jug on.'

'Righto.'

Selina followed Vera to the back of the laundromat and went up the rickety stairs which were dotted randomly with bits of carpet. She walked gingerly, worried more about her ankles than anything else. The psychiatrist had changed to a Paul Kelly album. 'Tell him to turn that bloody racket down—I'll mind your hat-box,' Vera shouted after her.

'At least he has taste in music,' Selina thought, as she knocked on the only door in sight on the first-floor landing. She heard a mysterious scratching noise on the other side, and began to wonder whether she was, after all, entirely safe. The door opened slightly and something hit her at about knee level. She fell over.

She had been hit by a blue heeler in a black collar studded with false jewels, who was now licking her face and standing on her hair; if anything, it was probably an improvement in style.

'Heeeerarrgh! Get way back!' she roared.

Rolf, the blue heeler, got a terrible shock. He hadn't been spoken to like that since he was a puppy on the farm. He bolted down the stairs to the landing and sat stock still, looking at Selina with his head on one side. She sat on the floor trying to get her hair out of her face, and looked back at him.

And that's how Jock Jovanovich, Serbo-Scottish psychiatrist, found them when he poked his head

21

round the door to see what was going on. He looked down at Selina. She looked up at him. Rolf looked at them both, but this time he tilted his head the other way.

This is what Selina saw: a tall bloke in horn-rimmed glasses who would pass for a Mills and Boon hero any day (dark, dangerously handsome, frowning, you know the drill), except for the fact that he was wearing the most lurid lime-green Hawaiian shirt imaginable, a purple party hat set at what could, unfortunately, only be described as a rakish angle, faded jeans and fluffy blue slippers exactly the same as Dot's.

'Don't be ridiculous,' Selina told herself. 'Far too handsome. Bound to be up himself and lazy in love as well.'

'Absurd,' Jock thought. 'She doesn't even have a hair-style.'

What Rolf saw were two human beings who were telling themselves silently and fervently that there was no such thing as love at first sight and for heaven's sake get a grip on yourself. Not that Rolf was aware of this, because although blue heelers are extremely smart, it is not in them to fathom the complexities of romance. Which is a good thing really, or blue heelers would be in charge of the world and aimless cattle would be the order of the day.

'What have you done to my dog?' said Jock, at exactly the same time Selina said, 'What are you doing with Mum's slippers?' Then nobody said anything for a while.

'Come here, Rolf,' said Jock, who knew that dogs

22

were very good to talk to when you couldn't think of what to say to a human. He'd written an article on it for the *Australasian Journal of Psychiatry* and sent them a photograph of Rolf wearing the party hat, but they had returned it with a note saying, 'This does not quite fit our purposes at the moment'. Jock had framed the note as a brilliant comment on life in general and hung it on his office wall next to his qualifications.

Rolf hurtled up the stairs and sat on Jock's left foot.

'Sorry fella,' said Selina, scratching him behind the ears, 'but you're a boisterous thing.' She looked up at Jock and decided to get straight to the point. 'Who are you and what do you want?' she said.

'What a great line,' said Jock. 'It's nearly as good as "Follow that cab!".'

Selina gave him a very similar look to the one that had once caused her older brother to leave the farm immediately, bicycle to the station and get the train to Melbourne where he stayed for a week. Jock went a bit funny at the knees, but continued.

'I am Jock Jovanovich, of Serbo-Scottish lineage, consultant psychiatrist of Brunswick Street, Fitzroy. I am touting for business, which is entirely illegal, but you looked so miserable in the street I couldn't help it. I drive a Triumph Herald, I have been engaged in interior decoration during the course of the morning in my new office, and I am fond of hedges cut into the shape of animals. This is Rolf, my bluey; I'm bored, the volume control on the stereo is completely cactus, I put on this

23

absurd hat because I think it makes me look dashing and I thought it might cheer you up. And this is my new office.' He flung open the door.

'Starve the bloody lizards,' breathed Selina, because sometimes she did impressions of her dad, too. Jock Jovanovich's office was chock-a-block with serious weirdness, even for a psychiatrist's office. There was an inflatable Godzilla hanging from the ceiling, a luminous hot-pink full-sized skeleton in one corner, a red velveteen *chaise-longue* with tassles on its matching cushions and a row of pompons underneath.

The carpet was a swirl of colourful cabbage roses. The single window was letting in the sound of a tram rumbling up Brunswick Street, a stream of light which illuminated an enormous desk covered in papers, books and record covers, and a stiff breeze which was blowing most of the papers off the desk and into the air. There was a big fish tank with goldfish, green weedy stuff and purple rocks, a whole wall of bookshelves overflowing with most un-textbook like volumes, and two whole shelves, wall to wall, of records. The stereo, which sat on a big speaker, boomed out again.

Selina looked at his hat critically. 'It doesn't look at all fetching, it looks ridiculous,' she shouted.

'Really?' Jock shouted back, astonished. He was used to women thinking he looked perfectly charming, no matter what he had on his head. Usually he only had to put on the Boyish Smile or the Devastating Piercing Stare Plus Single Eyebrow Arch and they were gorn.

Selina stepped between a life-size plaster statue

of the Queen Mother wearing a sunshine yellow ostrich-feather hat (clearly from Vera's wardrobe), a large cactus in a pot, a waist-high pile of comics and a cocktail cabinet on wheels displaying a range of teacups and saucers, and kicked the stereo plug out of the wall.

'Do you want me to have a go at fixing it?' she asked, shaking a stray curl in the direction of the stereo.

'Can you?' said Jock.

'I don't know, I haven't had a look at it yet,' said Selina, sitting on the other speaker which was wedged in a corner beside a revolving globe.

'Well, what do you think, Rolfie my lad?' Jock said, lifting his left index finger slightly. Rolf nodded his head sharply and barked once. Then he ran over and leaned on one of Selina's red shoes, which was dangling a good foot above the ground.

'Extremely cute,' remarked Selina as she sprang off the speaker, 'but I cannot help suspecting a certain amount of . . . ' she looked down at Rolf sternly, 'collusion!' Rolf jumped back, affronted, and Selina picked up the amplifier and sat on the floor with it on her lap. Rolf curled up in front of her and gave a tragic, doggie sort of sigh.

Selina shook her head thoughtfully and probed for a pin. She found some fluff from the first-floor landing, a small piece of Mintie wrapper, and finally plucked out a loosened hairpin. 'How come you've got records, not CDs?' she said, as she screwed off the back panel of the amp.

'I'm just an old-fashioned sort of guy,' said Jock, with an airy wave of one hand and a Boyish Smile

25

which was entirely wasted. Selina was concentrating on the job at hand and showed no signs of being mesmerised whatsoever. 'Um, well, no, that's not true. I do like vinyl. Like this,' he said, patting an old barber's chair upholstered in a dalmation print. 'Most of the records I like will probably never make it to CD anyway.' Jock stretched out in the chair and watched Selina ferret around in his stereo system.

'You're lucky,' she said, pushing her hair out of her face for the seventh time. 'It's just a loose wire. Built-in obsolescence thwarted again.' She twirled in the last screw, replaced the unit, and smiled at Jock. 'That's gratis, pal, as long as you don't play any Billy Joel on it.'

'Are you *mad*?' said Jock intensely. 'Wash your mouth out! . . . Hey, you've been crying.'

'Eh?' said Selina.

'You've been crying. What's the matter?'

'Why don't I just help you tidy up your new office and then I can go and collect my washing from Vera,' she said.

'Because I've only just got the office looking exactly the way I want it. Look, I've seen you before. You walk down the street looking cheerful. Sometimes you even whistle. Or skip. But today you look terrible.'

'Oh, most dashing, I must say.'

'Don't interrupt. You look terrible because you don't have any joy any more—or at least, that's how it seems. You want to tell me about it? It's not personal, it's professional. This is what I do. I get paid for it. If it makes you feel better, you can pay me the standard fee.'

'All I have left between me and complete poverty is your standard fee and seventeen cents,' said Selina.

'Maybe I can fix it,' he said gently. 'I haven't had a look yet.'

Selina sighed. 'OK, Dr Kildare.' She dusted herself off and replaced her hairpin somewhere in the vicinity of her scalp. 'Why not? Where do you want me? Do I languish on the couch like Lillie Langtry, or sit in the haircut special?'

'Well,' said Jock, standing up, 'I'm going to sit at my desk, and you can sit where you like. There are tissues on the desk if you need another weep.'

Selina brandished a clean hanky.

He sat down in his revolving office chair, span it around to face the desk, and took out a dark green notebook and a fountain pen from a drawer. 'I'm going to take notes, Miss . . . ?'

'It's Ms.' Selina lay down on the couch and kicked her shoes off. Rolf rested his head on her left shin. 'No, it isn't, it's just Selina Plankton, with a *K*.'

'Get out of it,' said Jock, pen poised.

'It is so. The only Planktons in the Manangatang phone book, thank you very much.' She turned over and put her chin in her hands. Displaced, Rolf settled down again, unperturbed. 'Hey, shouldn't I be talking to a thingummy? I mean I'm not totally berserko, or anything.'

'Quite possibly you should be talking to a thingummy,' said Jock. 'What manner of thingummy did you have in mind? A priest whatsit, or a counsellor hoozy-bob?'

27

'A psychologist. A psychologist thingummy,' said Selina.

'Ah, yes. I may be a psychiatrist doover, but I can do the other stuff, too. OK?'

'OK, OK. Where do I start? Don't say at the beginning.'

'No, I never do. Why were you crying?'

'I was crying because I've lost my job, tomorrow I'm getting evicted, and I'm going to be sawn in half by somebody called Keith, and because I have only just found out that the bloke I was going out with is a poser and a weasel-dick and Mum and Dad are losing money on the wool price and Hetty's having trouble laying.'

'Maybe you'd better start at the beginning,' said Jock.

'I knew you were going to say that,' said Selina.

So she told him about everything, about Miranda moving away, about not knowing what she wanted to do next, and how she wouldn't go back to wool-classing in a pink fit, and he asked her about her family and the farm. He wrote some things in his notebook and Selina cried a bit from frustration when she told him about Briian and how it appeared fairly impossible to find a man who was prepared to fall in love and stay that way and be loyal and fabulous and smart and funny and love you in your track-suit pants . . . She felt a bit better then, even though she'd already told Miranda and Ky and run up an impossible bill on the telephone and didn't know how she was going to pay it. Lastly she told him she was pre-menstrual and had hardly slept all week worrying about everything.

Jock put a soul album on volume level one, and said he was going to have a think. Selina went to sleep.

Jock watched her sleeping for a while, and put on his thinking hat, which was white with Dubbo Senior Bowls Thirds emblazoned on the band. He also wore it to strike terror into the hearts of other drivers.

Vera was right, Jock was barking mad; not bad mad, just deeply peculiar; and impetuous, a characteristic inherited from both parents. Slobodan Jovanovich and Heather McDougall had caught each other's eye during the interval of a pantomime at Melbourne's Princess Theatre. Five minutes later they were having it off in the cloakroom. Before Jock had divided into four cells, Slobodan the mechanic had graciously accepted Heather's proposal of marriage. Heather was a traditionally-minded woman with basic secretarial skills.

Their only child had grown into a 'man about town' psychiatrist who was regarded by many of his colleagues with a suspicion as deep as his peculiarity. Jock was of the considered opinion that the bad mad should be locked up safely away from kindergartens and female pedestrians, but the people who were merely a nuisance to society got a pretty raw deal. Much of this philosophy came from his parents, who had both grown up in a village atmosphere, one in Serbian Prystina, the other in the dock area of Glasgow. In both places the locals looked after the wandering souls who didn't quite share the same level of reality.

Jock figured that it was a better idea than locking people up and shooting them chock-a-block with tranquillisers, making them wear badly-cut pyjamas and feeding them colourless vegies. Not all places were like that of course, but government cut-backs had to hit somewhere and most mental patients didn't vote, although this is by no means evident from Australian election results.

In other times Jock would have been called a 'lady-killer'. As it was, the girlie network simply labelled him 'The Pants Man' and thus, marked as a root-rat, he was finding it more difficult to get dates from girls in the know. Luckily for him, he was also charming company and the situation was not yet critical. He had a collection of one hundred and sixteen lurid shirts and a reasonable swag of patients in various places around Melbourne.

Jock specialised in people who thought they were somebody else. Currently on the books he had a Napoleon, Emily Pankhurst, the Prime Minister, Wanda Jackson, Jeanne d'Arc, Tolstoy, a pale young hippie who thought he was a New Guinean Highlander, a man who insisted on calling himself Hiram F. Doppelganger and professed to be a multi-millionaire entrepreneur on the invalid pension, and a few old dears who were, in the words of the profession, 'a bit past it'. Generally he was paid by relatives who were waiting to inherit estates. It was a lucrative and time-consuming job.

Jock was in a bit of a career slump, having decided that most people were not going to 'get better' and that being sedated wasn't much of an improvement. As a university student he had wanted to 'cure people', or at least make life bearable for them. He knew he'd helped his patients, all of whom had become crack Trivial Pursuit players under Jock's rules of 'most inventive answer wins', but in the cure department, it had been a slack few years.

So he sat and thought in his thinking hat. He thought that Selina was gorgeous, and that she showed admirable impetuosity in spending her last $60 on a whim. He grinned. He took off the hat and began humming 'Cool Jerk' along with the stereo. Selina woke up, blinked a few times at the King Kong mobile swaying above her head, and asked, 'So what's the verdict, Kildare?'

Jock swung his feet off the desk. 'There's not a lot wrong with you except a really bad week, a mongrel ex-boyfriend and no money to speak of. Mostly I can't help people get away from their problems, I can only help them to cope better.' Jock slid a longish notebook over to himself and began writing on it. 'Maybe this will help you.' He signed his name and tore off one of the sheets.

Selina walked up to his desk and leaned over it. 'If that is a prescription for tranquillisers, Dr Kildare . . . ' she whispered, 'then you are a contemptible quack and I am going to trash your stereo.' Rolf put his head between his paws and shut his eyes. Jock looked at Selina. Selina looked at Jock.

Jock handed Selina a crossed personal cheque for $10 000.

I Suppose Falling in Love is Out of the Question

Selina could take a joke. She took the cheque to the bank. The teller looked at the cheque and was saying it would take a few days to clear and did she have any ID and was it a pay cheque and what was her mother's maiden name and who won the last US Open, when he was called away by a boss in a grey suit for a whispered consultation.

The teller went and sat down at a desk called Inquiries and the boss came over and smiled at Selina with the lower half of his face.

'What?' she asked.

'We've just had a call from Dr Jovanovich. I can authorise immediate clearance for cash, Ms Planktonne.'

'Well fuck me,' thought Selina, because

sometimes she did impressions of her Aunty Gail but usually not out loud.

'How would you like it?' asked the suit.

'Excuse me?'

'Your cash, madam. How would you like it?'

'I'd like it a lot,' said Selina. 'Can I open an account?'

Could she ever.

And could she add some liquidity to her dessicated credit-card account?

Well, was the Pope a bloke?

Selina went over to Keith's to tell him her ridiculous story. She planned to go home and cuddle up with her hot-water bottle, which had a natty little Footscray jumper, courtesy of Dot, but Keith never wasted a rehearsal opportunity.

Selina and Keith had practised The Divided Woman many times before, aiming to perform it at a special Christmas show. Christmas had come two weeks early, and with only a week's solid practice, Selina was a little nervous. The Great Salami would have been happier with more rehearsal time but it seemed to be coming along fairly well.

After a solid three hours of run-throughs with The Great Salami in his fibro garage, she had one last cup of tea before leaving.

'I know this saw looks pretty wimpy,' said Keith,

'but the chainsaw's cactus. I took the liberty of ringing up your Dad, Boops, and he's sending down his double-handed saw on tonight's train. I'll get someone from the audience to do the other end, OK?'

Selina nodded.

'No worries,' said Keith. 'I'll pick the saw up from the freight office tonight. And tomorrow, rehearsal four o'clock, show-time ten.'

'Right you are, kabana-face. See you there.'

On the way to the tram stop, she saw the lurid posters advertising their last performance at the Zippo Club. There was a terrible line-drawing of a buxom woman screaming as she was threatened with a chainsaw. Selina rolled her eyes. When she got home, cheered slightly by a short burst of 'Good-night Irene' from the burly tram conductor as she alighted, she found the front door open.

'If you're a burglar,' she shouted down the hallway of her flat, 'come out here and take it like a man! I'm going to knock your . . .'

'Language! Anyway, I'm a girlie burglar!' came the reply. It was Dot, blue slippers and all, coming down to meet her daughter and wiping her hands on her pinny on the way. 'Hello Sellie, you poor old love, you look done in. I've put the roast on, and your dad's reading in the lounge.'

Selina was enveloped in a hug. 'I don't know, Mum, sometimes this family's just like a margarine commercial.'

'Except that your father's reading *Fat is a Feminist Issue*. What sort of a day have you had, dear? We thought we'd come and cheer you up, and have a gander at your last show with young Keith. He rang us about the saw, and we decided to bring it down ourselves. I nearly bought you one of those awful ironing board covers with the naked bloke on it. I thought it would be an improvement on what's-his-face.'

When she'd stopped laughing, deposited the hat-box, given her dad a kiss on his bald spot, and rung The Great Salami to tell him the double-handed saw was already in town, Selina sat down at the table and explained to her mum and dad how some joker had given her $10 000.

'This isn't something to do with Rothwells, is it?' said Len, suspiciously.

'That was years ago, Dad. No, I think he's a loony.'

'He can't be a loony, Sellie, he's a doctor. Does he want to get into your knickers, do you think?'

'Mum! I don't know. Probably. But it's not conditional on the cheque, it's already cleared and in my name at the Commonwealth in Brunswick Street. Whadderyereckon?'

'I think he's a loony,' said Len.

'I think he wants to get into your knickers,' said Dot.

Then talk turned to The Divided Woman, they had roast lamb, and Len oiled the saw in front of an SBS documentary on the Penan people of the Malaysian rainforest.

'Any bastard should realise they're cutting down too many of those trees,' said Len. 'Greed, that's all it is, Mum.'

'You're not wrong, Len,' replied Dot. 'I'll make you a Horlicks, Sellie.'

'I haven't got any.'

'I brought some down in a little jar. The only things I ever find in your fridge are science experiments. Off to bed with you, Len, we've got the bloody Art Gallery in the morning, and you'll want to be back for "This Sporting Life" on the wireless.'

For the first time in almost a week, Selina had a good, long sleep.

Saturday 12 December 1998

By 9.55 pm the following night, the Zippo Club was hot to trot. There were festoons of coloured lights winking in the gloom and streamers in primary colours draped over the rafters. The pensioners had come out in force, ordering Pimms instead of shandies as a farewell gesture. The support act, a fire-eater called Dolores del Brunswick, had lit a line of one hundred and fifty sambucas on the bar and frightened the bejeezus out of O'Toole in the process. Ky, the Mgambls and the Planktons were massed at a front table, and Briian the Crazed Architect was nursing a boutique beer and a filthy temper at the back, near the bar.

At 9.57 pm, a tall, absurdly handsome man in horn-rimmed glasses threaded his way to the front table and bagged the last chair in the place, which Selina had vacated twenty minutes earlier. Briian could see him introduce himself, and Selina's parents look at each other meaningfully. How dare she dump him before he dumped her? And who was this low-life in his tasteless purple shirt with green polka dots? Briian was too intent on perving to notice a small blue heeler shoot between people's legs and under the bloke's chair.

Briian ordered a triple Bundy and Coke. Wayne, the enormous Kiwi bouncer who looked like a nightmare in a tuxedo, but had a heart of tapioca, cracked his scarred knuckles and completed a technically questionable drum roll with two rulers on the stage floor.

'Lideeez and Gennelmen!' he shouted, as the place quietened down a bit. 'Intro-douching . . . for the first time uvver at the world-famous Zuppo Club . . . the uncredible Divided Wummen! This daring performance, unparalleled in the modern EE-posh, wull be undertaking by The Ger-ate Salami!'

The Great Salami swept on stage to thunderous applause. Keith had outdone himself. Over white gloves, borrowed from Dot at the last moment because Keating had made an impromptu snack of his own, and tuxedo, he was wearing a purple velvet cape that looked to O'Toole suspiciously like the curtain from the Zippo Club office—but perhaps this was not the time to bring it up.

Wayne wheeled out the apparatus. It looked a bit like a skinny kitchen table with a long plywood trunk on top of it. The trunk had hinged lids on the top and big, red, spangly stars and glitter scattered over the green paint left over after Keith did his back fence last summer. It had been copied out of one of the more antique volumes from The Great Salami's magic library and slimmed down for the modern age and Selina, who was a little shorter than the magician's assistant in the book.

Wayne bowed, and took up his bouncer's position once more.

'On ya Wayne!' said the pensioners, ordering more Pimms.

'Good evening my lovely audience,' began Keith, his hands clasped together rather demurely. 'I see you are looking at my impressive apparatus.' His eyebrows wiggled wildly, and there were a few titters from the more clued-up women in the front row.

'Keep it clean, Salami old mate!' shouted Len from the front row, earning him a shove from Dot and a beer from Jock.

'My verld famous apparatus is for the special performance zis evenink of The Divided Woman! And to assist me in this magical, and incerrr-rrredibly dangerous performance, my beeyoodiful assistant, Boopsie!' The Great Salami flung his right arm high into the air and twirled his cape around a bit. Selina entered stage left.

'Oooooooh,' said everybody, except Rolf, who couldn't see.

Selina looked wonderful. Everybody said so. Dot had always known that hot pink lurex at the back of the linen press would come back into fashion one day, even though there wasn't much of it. Following the pattern for a French maid's uniform for a fancy-dress party she had cut out of the

Women's Weekly in 1967 and filed in the barn, under H for High-jinks, Dot had created a hot-pink bodice appliquéd with red stars (on advice from Keith during a secret telephone call), a tiny skirt in green horse-blanket supported by a series of stiff, tulle petticoats originally white, but sprayed gold with the paint she had left over from doing the ping-pong balls for the tree last Christmas. It was, as Len had pronounced early on in the piece, a treat. Selina had teamed the fabulous creation with gold fish-net tights, a present from The Great Salami, who had paid $3.50 for them in the front bar of the Pedestrian from a seedy character who was escorted from the premises shortly afterwards. Red shoes, of course, and a riotous back-combed hair-do topped it all off, if you don't count the tiara. As Selina came to a stop with arms elegantly outstretched, and gave one hand to The Great Salami, her tiara, which was actually Porkie and Beth, flew into the air.

'Ahhhhhh,' said everybody.

'Ow,' said Selina, because Beth had bits of Selina's fringe in her toes.

The audience gave Selina a charming round of applause and she bowed deeply, dislodging three hairpins and some unidentified fluff.

'My beeyoodiful assistant, Boopsie, will enter the apparatus, and I will saw her in half!' announced The Great Salami, with a flourish.

The crowd leaned closer, smoke filling the air, the only lights a twenty-five-watter over the bar and the spotlights. Briian began to stagger towards the stage.

'Mr Wayyyyyne!' commanded The Great Salami, his eyes rolling wildly, 'Fetch me . . . the SAW!'

Len stood up and took off his jacket. Underneath he was wearing a navy-blue singlet emblazoned with 'Manangatang Double-Handed Sawing Handicap Champ'. His strange chopping muscle stood out on his right shoulder as he picked up a beautifully-made oak box, long like a billiard cue case. 'Here you go Wayney,' he said. 'Look after me saw.'

Wayne carried it carefully to Selina, and they took one end each. The Great Salami opened the four brass clasps, snap! snap! snap! snap! and whipped out the saw. It was long and silver and shining, with well-worn hardwood handles and wicked teeth.

Everyone gasped.

Suddenly, there was a kerfuffle at the front of the stage, near the Mgambl-Plankton table. Briian was shaking a Kahlua and milk up into the lights. 'That's not a bloody saw. It's fake! This whole thing's bullshit! It's done with mirrors! Heaps of bloody mirrors!'

Wayne and Selina knew just how to handle this sort of occasion. They'd once done a workshop with Circus Oz, and had learned some extremely handy skills.

'Hoopla!' Wayne said to Selina under his breath. She braced herself and nodded.

'Eeek!' shouted Wayne, 'A bloody yuppie! HAAAALP!' and threw himself into Selina's arms. It brought the house down.

They took a bow together. When their heads

40

were about knee level (respectively) he whispered, 'You want me to hut him, Sel?'

'Nah,' she replied. 'Your knuckles are prettier than his face. Save 'em.'

As they straightened, The Great Salami struck the saw with a hammer. It made a satisfying sound (that kind of went, KERRRANGGGG, if you want an approximation) which pretty much indicated that the saw was not made of rubber.

'Zis special saw,' he said, 'Belongs to Mr Len Plankton, winner of several sings, including, correct me if I go wrong here, Miz-sewer Plankton, ze Open Invitation Combination Handicap Relay Three Hundred Millimetre Underhand, Standing Block and Tree Felling Golden Axe Prize at ze Royal Show only a few short years ago!'

'My oath!' shouted Len.

'Arrrrgh, crap,' said Briian, taking a swig of Joseph Mgambl's mineral water and spitting it out.

Wayne had come off the stage and put a vast hand on Briian's shoulder. The radio microphone on his lapel picked up and broadcast to the audience Briian's next mumbled comment.

'How 'bout a Black Russian for Mr Coon?' he sneered as he dug Wayne in the hip with his elbow. A hush fell over the Zippo. Briian, needless to say, didn't notice. A low growl came up from somewhere near Joseph's boots. His wife laid a restraining hand on his shoulder.

'Shut up, Rolf,' hissed Jock.

'Kill the yuppie!' shouted Mrs Mavis Deaming (ret.), president of the bowling club and a dab hand at crochet if she did say so herself. Her compatriots shouted approval. Several members of the Essendon Football Club cheer squad, mindful of an Aboriginal player who had kicked the winning goal for them in the last finals series, started a slow hand clap.

Wayne reached out with one smooth motion and tossed Briian on to the stage. Leaving him to collect his wits, which didn't take long even when he wasn't pissed, Wayne relieved The Great Salami of the saw and leaned against the apparatus to watch.

'What haf we here?' asked Keith, who was in dire need of an accent coach.

'Is zis ze white man's burden?' He plucked at Briian's red braces, which were holding up his expensive bottle-green baggy trousers. Keith patted Briian's crotch. 'Not much of a burden here, ladies,' he winked. 'Ziz man has no apparatus to speak of!' Briian was beginning to sober up a bit under the lights and the collective derision.

The Great Salami made a flew flourishes and implored the audience, 'Tell me, my friends, is zis the future of the Zippo Club? Is zis a healthy man? Let me feel your glands!' Keith pressed his fingers into Brian's neck, and felt his forehead. 'Is there a doctor in ze house?' he asked, alarmed.

'I'm a doctor!' said Jock, standing up.

Momentarily thrown—as the question had never been answered in the affirmative in his entire career—The Great Salami inquired, 'What's wrong with this man?'

'He's a dickhead,' said Jock. Dot looked at him.

The Great Salami continued. 'Is zis a wealthy

42

man, perhaps? Let us see!' He walked away from Briian, and took a wallet out of his pocket. 'Oh look, an American Express gold card!'

Briian lunged for it.

'Give me that! You've got no right!' Briian's knees felt suddenly chilly. The audience roared as he fell over. He realised something was up; and it wasn't his trousers.

The Great Salami twirled his cape, produced Briian's red braces and commanded, 'Don't leave home without them.'

Wayne scooped up Briian and his braces, and carried him through the crowd to the bar. The show would go on. Wayne leaned close to Briian and said, very quietly, 'Sellie says I'm not supposed to hut you in the face. But that's prutty specific.'

Wayne ordered a mineral water and a bottle of champagne, and dived back into the crowd. He deposited the champagne in front of Jock, and the mineral water in front of Joe. 'Mr Mgambl,' he said, 'I'd like to apologise for thet incident happening in this club'.

Joe smiled a little. 'It happens everywhere, old son. Thank you.'

'Mirrors?' The Great Salami was saying, in a very high voice. 'Zis performance of The Divided Woman is magic, one of the sacred secrets of our ancient craft! I invite members of ze audience to inspect ze apparatus for hidden mirrors or any other tricky little schemy fiddle faddle! And ze saw! Ze saw of ze great Len Plankton, hero to wood-shopping folk in small Tasmanian towns!' A few people tramped up on stage, and The Great Salami

43

opened the catches of the long box, spinning the apparatus around on its castors. It was inspected, patted, knocked, and pronounced plywood. As well as being open at the top, it was divided in the middle, marked by a line and a couple of catches so it could be pulled apart, later. But all in all, just a plywood box.

'Now, ladies and gentlemen, we go on! Boopsie, please!'

The Great Salami invited Wayne back on to the stage to pick up Selina gracefully and deposit her at one end of the box. Selina walked to the other end of the box, holding Keith's hand for balance as she went. She extended one foot at a time, elegantly, and kicked each red shoe to the ground. Wayne made a funny noise with a cowbell off-stage when each shoe hit the ground.

Selina lay down in the box, her head protruding from one end, and her feet from the other. She kicked her legs so that the audience would see they were really her extremities, and settled them back. Her head rested on a small wooden plank with some foam padding. The Great Salami flounced around the box once, shouting 'Are you ready, my dear Boopsie! Are you sure you can do this, my brave leetle compañera?' He turned to the audience. 'Should she do this? Risk her life, for magic?!'

Everyone seemed to think so.

The Great Salami closed the lids on each half of the box, bang! bang! and fastened the catches securely. Two members of the Essendon cheer squad confirmed their authenticity, and left the

44

stage to applause. Selina's head and feet were the only things visible. She turned slowly towards the audience, with a horrified expression on her face. Dot was looking at her, but knitting under the table, her dad was looking proud, but also a little concerned, his eyes not quite on hers. Obviously Keith had picked up his best saw again.

'I need a volunteer to take the other handle and help me saw the lady in half! Any volunteers, while I take her for a spin?'

Keith wheeled Selina around in a circle, so the audience could see the other side of the box. When Selina had first tried the box it had seemed claustrophobic, but now it was just snug, and a bit weird. She felt divorced from her feet, as if there were nothing in between.

Nobody was game to take on the wicked saw, so Len was urged to go up. 'I don't want to cut me daughter in half!' he protested, but up he went anyway.

'Boopsie's daddy will help me perform ze Divided Woman! Sacre Groove Thang!'

Wayne hit the tape deck, and 'The Flight of the Bumble Bee' blared out. The crowd craned their necks to see as The Great Salami fitted the saw into the tiny crack between each half of the apparatus. Len took the upstage end, The Great Salami raised one hand, and Selina screamed.

'WAIT!' The music stopped.

Every eye in the place snapped to her head.

'Does my hair look OK?'

'Boopsie! You look beeyoodiful!'

'OK, then, I'm ready.'

45

The music and the tension returned, The Great Salami shouted, 'GO!' and he and Len went at it, hell for leather. Len's back started to glisten with sweat, his chopping muscle standing out crazily on his shoulder blade. All the while, Selina was madly winking at Jock, part of the act, but fun all the same. Up the back, Briian glowered.

Finally, the saw reached the bottom of the apparatus. It must have gone right through her! Len wiped his forehead while Keith produced two large chopping blades with wooden handles. He rotated one carefully for the crowd to see, then pushed it down between the two halves so only its handle protruded at the top. He grabbed the other, rotating it, too, and slid it neatly into the same gap, then undid the clips at the bottom holding the halves of the box together.

Suddenly, and dramatically, he pulled the box apart. The half with Selina's head went west. The half with her feet went east.

'Ohhhhhhhhh,' said everybody, Mavis fell off her chair, and the applause went on while The Great Salami spun each half around by itself. Selina felt very strange, such a long way from the ground in one direction, and her feet in the other. There seemed to be no feeling in her legs. She missed her body, no matter what *Cleo* magazine might have to say about her thighs.

The Great Salami turned the boxes around, each with a bit of Selina at one end and a big cleaver at the other, until her head and her feet met up in the middle of the stage, about a metre apart.

'Signor Plantone!' he shouted. 'Are these your daughter's feet?'

Len strolled over. The audience held their breath. Len pulled off a red shoe and tweaked Selina's big toe. 'This little piggy . . .' he began.

Selina began to laugh uncontrollably. 'Dad! Stop! You know I can't stand it!'

'Works every time,' said Len.

One more time around, and The Great Salami put the two halves back together, clipped them at the bottom, took out the choppers, undid the clasps and flipped the lid open. The audience strained to see into the box. Selina kicked her feet high, stood up and took a neat swan dive into Wayne's arms. He held her as if carrying a surfboard, then lowered her feet to the ground and scuttled off.

Selina and The Great Salami took a low bow, joined for a second one by Len. The three of them held hands high in the air and as one, accepted the standing ovation by almost scraping the ground with their noses and doing in Len's back.

There were calls for more, but it's a bit hard to top the old Divided Woman act, so The Great Salami made a short speech of thanks, and brought Porkie and Beth and Keating on stage to say goodbye. Then O'Toole announced that the new Zippo Club would open again in two weeks' time with pink and grey carpet and mirrors on the walls, and was booed for his trouble.

After a while, Keith and Selina came out front in their civvies and accepted congratulations and drinks from well-wishers. Selina and Ky shared a chair, and Dot put her knitting away and led a rousing chorus of 'For they are jolly good fellows', interrupting Len and Jock's disagreement about Charles Aznavour's use of adjectives.

Later, the Planktons retrieved their belongings from the Zippo cloakroom. Len and Dot had decided to park their caravan out the back of the Mgambls' place; Selina had three hat-boxes and no fixed address, as of that afternoon. There were lots of hugging goodbyes, and Selina promised to tell her parents when she had decided what to do with the next bit of her life.

'You'll be right,' said Len, as he headed off with Dot and Kylie. 'Make sure she gets home safely, Wayne—wherever that is.'

Wayne nodded. 'Yeah, I'll just lock up first. You can stay at my place,' he offered. 'Trent's away, on a modelling shoot, and I can sleep on the couch.' Jock looked at him thoughtfully.

'I know,' she said, smiling. 'Thanks.'

Suddenly, a crumpled Briian emerged from the darkened Zippo, and staggered towards Selina.

'Hey you,' he slurred.

'Oh, for God's sake,' said Selina.

'Who's your new *boy*friend?' he said, waving an arm at Jock.

'He's not my boyfriend,' said Selina.

'Good, then how about a goodnight kiss?' Briian lurched towards Selina.

'Oh dear,' she sighed.

Selina turned into a blur, sidestepping Briian, and appearing behind him.

48

He turned and came at her again, angry now, and gripped her arm, hard.

Jock looked at Wayne, then Selina, and moved forward, but Wayne put a hand on his shoulder. 'No, mate. She's all right.'

'Let me go, Briian,' said Selina.

'You want it,' he slurred.

'Let me go, please.'

Briian bent over her, and shoved his face closer. Selina bowed again, just like on stage, only this time she didn't go so low. She hit Briian's nose with the part of her forehead near her hairline. Brian sat down on the footpath in amazement, holding his nose.

'You've broken it!' he howled.

'No I haven't, you big sook.'

They left him there and strolled along the street towards Wayne's ute. 'He's definitely in with a chance, then, Sellie?' Wayne remarked.

'Could go close to an engagement,' agreed Selina.

As the three people and one blue heeler drove off, their last image of Briian was of a dishevelled man trying to dial on his mobile phone, in a phone box on Smith Street.

Jock and Rolf had graciously accepted Wayne's offer of a cup of tea and a biscuit, although Rolf was clearly keener on the biscuit, and Jock was clearly keener on Selina.

When they arrived, Selina stacked her hat-boxes in one corner of the room and collapsed on the couch, demanding tea and sympathy. Wayne provided the tea, Rolf licked her hand, and they all sat up for a couple of hours talking about what

49

she could do with $10 000. The suggestions had reached the entirely ludicrous stage when Wayne stretched. He brought out some sheets, blankets and pillows, and retired to the bedroom, after shaking hands with Jock and scratching Rolf behind his ears. He kissed Selina on the top of her head (Wayne was courageous) and requested scrambled eggs for breakfast.

Selina and Jock had another cup of tea, and Rolf went to sleep under the coffee table.

'Well,' said Jock, 'in the normal course of events, I suppose I should proposition you or go home. But I don't want to go home because I like talking to you, and I can't proposition you because I've given you some money and it wouldn't be proper.'

'I suppose we should talk about the money. Do you want it back?'

'No, it's yours now. What are you going to do?'

'I don't know. I feel a bit lost. Oh!' Selina stopped languishing on the couch and sat up straight.

'What time is it?'

'About three.'

'I forgot to ring Miranda! I promised I would, after the show.'

Selina grabbed Wayne's banana-shaped phone and dialled the Darwin number hoping Miranda would still be awake. She was.

'Hi, mate ... yeah ... Reality Checks our Special ... Shit. Shit. Shit. What do you mean?' asked Selina. Jock watched her face furrow in concern.

'He can't get you sacked can he?' Selina listened some more. 'It sounds like the Wild West up there.

No, don't cry, I'll come and help you. I know. I know. I love you too. No, no, it's a very long story but I got $10 000 . . . from a man. No, I did not have to do any snorkelling to get it . . .'

'Snorkelling?' Jock said to Rolf.

'Are they still there? I'll get on the next plane possible. God, I had no idea things got so bad. Yes. Now keep everything locked. I'll ring you with the flight number. Mmm. See you. I'll be there in a minute.'

Selina's face was pale, much paler than when Briian had confronted her.

'What the hell was that?' said Jock.

'Miranda's in trouble. I have to go to Darwin in the morning.'

'Pardon?'

'Shut up for a minute,' said Selina firmly, dialling again. There was a flight to Darwin in three and a half hours. She booked herself on it, and hung up.

'Apparently she's going to Darwin,' Jock said to Rolf.

She dialled again. 'M? You OK? Get a grip on yourself. I'm coming in on the 1.20 afternoon flight. Australian Airlines 22. Now ring somebody beefy and get them to come over until I get there. No. Now. It will make *me* feel better. You'll sort it out, and I'll have a holiday. Yep, see ya. And get some sleep.'

Jock looked at Rolf. 'Darwin. Today.'

She hung up again and turned to Jock. 'Miranda's in trouble. Some Minister for Sleaze threatened to get her sacked and when that didn't work he sent

51

two thugs in a car around to scare her. They're sitting outside her place in a Commodore.'

'What does it matter what kind of car they're driving?'

'I don't know. Sometimes you hang on to details when the rest of the weirdness doesn't make any sense.'

'Why doesn't she call the cops?'

'Because the Minister for Sleaze is also the Minister for Cops. And it seems, intimidating our Lois Lane. I've never heard her so spooked before. So I'm going. Where are my shoes?'

Jock turned to Rolf. 'Darwin,' he said, 'it's in the Northern Territory.'

'Miranda and me have been friends since we were four years old. She's pulled me out of a river and a car full of out-of-town would-be rapists. Me, Ky and Miranda are like sisters. I don't have to go, but I want to go. And you've given me the means to do it. Otherwise I'd just be sitting here going out of my mind with worry. This way, even if it gets sorted out in a couple of days, I can maybe find a job, have a holiday, keep her company for a while. I'm not supposed to be depressed, remember?'

'Me and my big chequebook,' he said.

So Jock caught a taxi and went to pick up his car while Selina wrote a note to Wayne explaining why he wasn't going to get breakfast in bed, and a long letter to her parents, and to Ky. She had a shower, changed into her sun-frock and put stockings under it and a jumper over it, which she could whip off before she hit the northern heat.

On the way to the airport in Jock's Triumph Herald, which was ten years older than Selina, he kept up a running commentary about how to escape from crocodiles and men with beer guts in Commodores, and made Selina laugh. In fact, they both laughed so much that when Jock pulled into the temporary car-park at the airport and turned off the engine, they both looked at each other with some regret.

'I suppose falling in love is out of the question?' said Jock.

Selina didn't say anything.

'Will you write to me?'

'OK.' She smiled at him. 'Will you write back?'

'I'm not very good at that sort of thing,' he said. 'I'll tell you what, Kildare, we'll stick to postcards.'

'Couldn't I just come with you?'

No he couldn't. Selina paid for her ticket with reactivated plastic, checked her luggage and got her seat allocation, and kissed him goodbye, which made four knees go all sort of woozy. He said, 'Be careful,' then she flew out of his life.

That was the plan, anyway.

Come On, Miranda

Selina slept when she could during the seven-hour flight, interrupted mostly by meals and toxic-looking refresher towelettes provided by the airline steward, who sneaked her a free vodka and tonic to make up for the whingeing plastic-pipe salesman who had bored her witless since Adelaide, and who had, fortunately, departed in Alice Springs.

After she had brought her seat into the upright position because they would shortly be arriving in Darwin, and secured her tray table and looked out on to a sparkling blue harbour, Selina collected her jumper and stockings from the overhead locker and stepped out into a wall of soggy heat.

She walked across the hot tarmac. To her right,

54

through a cyclone-wire fence, she could see war planes at the RAAF base. Just inside the door of the terminal was a slightly haggard Miranda. There was only time for a quick appraisal before she was pounced upon and hugged tight. Selina could feel her friend's ribs through the cotton singlet. She pulled away, reached up to ruffle Miranda's blond, spiky haircut and spoke their customary greeting, a private joke which originated from the now deceased Manangatang postmaster of their youth. 'Hello there young girlie, get out of it.'

'Gee, it's good to see you.'

'Are you all right, bloss?'

'Yairs. Right as rain. Well, not really. Bit tired. Come and get your stuff and tell me about your news and I'll fill you in at home. The thug brigade left early this morning.'

They walked arm in arm to the luggage carousel.

'How long can you stay?'

'For a while, I think. Maybe get a job . . . I dunno.'

'Well, we'll sort it out later. Your hat-box I presume?' While they waited for the others, Selina took time to look around. The building was open at one end for air flow, and big ceiling fans turned lazily. People were greeting new arrivals, getting ready to leave, booking charter flights; there were black faces and brown faces and Asian faces, and the bright pink faces of tourists who'd come at the wrong time of year and were going home to cooler places and hangover cures.

There were men and women in Australian military uniform, armed and languorous. It felt like another country. Now she understood why

Miranda joked about being a 'foreign correspondent'. It wasn't just the distance, it was the feel.

The drive to Miranda's, in her physically challenged Hillman Minx, reinforced the sense of being in another world. The light was so harsh. The tropical gardens were full of frangipani and bougainvillea, and palm trees—tall, squat, and untidy. There were houses on stilts and other houses which looked like fibro bunkers with bits of air-conditioner sticking out the front, and a lot of utes on the road with people in the back. In Melbourne, even dogs weren't allowed in the back of utes.

As they passed a big, vastly ugly building with CASINO writ large on its fortress front, she saw a group of Aboriginal women in pretty, floral dresses playing cards under a tree. They were laughing. They were also the most modestly dressed people Selina had seen in thirty minutes. Everybody else was showing a lot of flesh: shoulders, legs, backs, chests, and feet. People in the street were dressed as if they were at the beach. Even Miranda, usually dressed in a uniform of jeans and long-sleeved shirt, was wearing khaki okanuis and thongs.

An insipid pop song on the car radio was followed by an announcement in a deep, mellifluous voice, that this was not a cyclone warning but we were in the cyclone season and people should be prepared but repeat, this was not a cyclone warning. Suddenly a car swerved in front of Miranda and turned sharp left.

'Pissed,' said Miranda, succinctly.

'But it's only just lunch-time,' protested Selina.

'Precisely,' Miranda replied. 'Welcome to Darwin, hon.'

Miranda's house, surrounded by palm, frangipani and pawpaw trees, looked over the sea at Nightcliff, from the top of tall steel pylons. The house had banks of louvre windows instead of weatherboards, all around the outside. The louvres, always left open to catch the breezes, were covered in a thin layer of dust. Selina calculated that a floor to ceiling dusting job would probably take a couple of days. Each room was equipped with a ceiling fan, and handwoven mats from Arnhem Land were scattered about the wooden floor.

'Three-up?' asked Miranda, which meant 'tea' in a private language of long-term friendship, with its forgotten etymology and phrases like 'Do we know him?' and 'Do we like her?' Selina wanted a siesta first, so Miranda gave her the house tour and then left her to the spare bedroom, where Selina collapsed on the low futon under a pink mosquito net for a few hours. She dozed, unused to sleeping without the heaviness of pyjamas and a doona, and dreamed about Rolf eating Briian's trousers. When she woke up, she wrapped one of Miranda's blue sarongs around herself, went to the kitchen, and made a jug of iced lemon cordial which she took out to her old friend on the verandah.

There was no breeze and although the ice in the jug melted within five minutes, they stayed outside for a long time, enjoying the sort of ridiculously-large-orange-sun-against-purple-clouds view which makes Northern Territory sunset postcards look fake. Miranda, as usual rising from a sea of newspapers and magazines and sucking on a paper cut from an *Independent Monthly* subscription card, tried to explain how she had attracted the unwelcome attention of shadowy figures driving big white cars. Selina could feel the sweat sliding down the back of her knees.

'It's stupid,' Miranda began. 'It's kind of like some really dumb movie with bad actors in it. I did this voice piece for last Monday morning's current affairs show about the Zoning Minister Harold Franklin. He's the Deputy Premier, the sort of red-neck bastard that reporters are s'posed to respect. He's a 24-stone former Olympic weightlifter with a red toupée he forgets to wear. And he's got a tattoo of the storming of the Winter Palace at Versailles on his back. He's a big media favour-ite. They all know he's a raving racist ratbag—that sounds good, wish I could use it—but they never say it. He has a reputation for putting his foot in his mouth, but generally he gets away with it. Anyway, I'd been covering a dinner he spoke at the Saturday before, and he made all these comments about Aboriginal people. Not during the speech, but talking to these mining executives afterwards. I was standing nearby, waiting to get a sound grab. You know, just thirty seconds I could use for Monday morning. Anyway, he said all this gross stuff to them about how the Government would be happy to back the mining company trying to get an exploration licence on Aboriginal land. Nothing too unusual in that, but he described the local community as "just a bunch of coons".'

'He *what*?' said Selina, thinking that someone else had used that word recently.

'Amazing isn't it? Yes, and what's more went on to explain his scientific theories. You think he'd know better. Anyway, he ranted on about people coming down from the trees, and the missing link—it was lovely stuff,' said Miranda.

'Oh, come off it, M, people don't talk like that any more unless they're crazed architects.'

'What?' said Miranda.

'Nothing. But he must have been joking. Not very funny, I know, but surely . . . '

'Look,' said Miranda, 'I'm telling you straight. This place is wild. So, the upshot is, I did a voicer about his personal style, and said at the end, "And any Minister of the Crown who can get away with calling his Aboriginal constituents 'coons', as Mr Franklin did after Saturday's formal dinner, is certainly somebody to watch". Not a particularly pretty sentence, but I did record it at half-past six in the morning.

'Anyway, the Government starts screaming blue murder, Franklin releases categorical denial, the local Murdoch rag goes berserk about hotbed of radical lefties at the ABC and Franklin demands that Fingle—that's my chief of staff—give me the boot. So of course, I had to drag out the tape.'

'Tape.'

'Yeah, well, you know me, always an eye for the main chance. A bit unethical perhaps, coz obviously Franklin didn't know it was on. I said I was doing a sound check while I waited. I was standing behind him, so he didn't see it. And of course, it's a bit indistinct when you don't get the mike right under their schnozz, but it's there all right.' Miranda noticed Selina's expression and said 'What's the matter?'

'Nothing. I've just got *déjà vu*. Go on.'

'Needless to say old Franklin had no idea, so he keeps up the denial. Even held what passes for a press conference up here. We kept saying we had a tape, he kept saying we didn't, and in the end we had to run it. So not only did the public find out about the coon crap, they got the full force of Mr Franklin's evolution theory as well.' Miranda set down her cordial and sighed.

'Would you believe, he said it was a fake. A conspiracy. That night somebody broke in here and took a whole heap of tapes. They got the original, but we had it on the master tape of the morning we broadcast it.

'Then I get three phone calls in the middle of the night telling me to leave town. Bloody subtle, I must say. Of course, I can't prove it was anybody connected with him. Then last night these two blokes sat out there in the look-out car-park until about four in the morning. Kind of strange though—they didn't look up here, just kept staring out at the water. I just got spooked, and you rang in the middle of it.

'Anyway, I can only hope it all just fades away. Up here, if you ask a question the slightest bit, I don't know, like not a PR question, they say you're a raving southern socialist. It's like Queensland fifteen years ago. It's bizarre. The local paper's idea of an investigative question is, "So, Minister, how will this help the public?" and then they shut up for five minutes while he reads the press release.'

Selina successfully averted a typical Miranda-tirade against the failing ethics of journalism by slapping at a mosquito and asking: 'So, are you in danger, d'you think?'

'I thought I was, but now that you're here, I think maybe I'm being a bit drama-queenie. It's just that . . . everything seems different up here. I don't know, like it's not even the same year as it is in other places. And it's so isolated. Seeing you is kind of a reminder that the outside world exists—apart from this stuff . . . ' She waved a magazine, then continued: 'So, I s'pose I should show you around. It's not all neanderthal. There's some really nice people, some fantastic Aboriginal art exhibitions, and music, and it's slower than Manangatang. It'll be a funny old Christmas. I hope the wet arrives before then.'

That night, Selina fell asleep to the chirrupy, clicking sounds of frail-looking geckos who ran all over her ceiling eating tiny insects, and to the fragrance of frangipani outside her wall of windows.

Melbourne, Sunday 13 December 1998

Jock and Rolf were working a weekend shift involving the usual rounds of patients. The man who thought he was Napoleon used to scare Rolf by insisting in regal tones that he attack the platoon

61

from the flank, but Rolf was used to it by now. The most pressing difficulty for Jock, apart from the fact that his latest liaison was talking about moving in with him (after one date), and he'd met a fabulous girl who had taken off for Darwin with his ten grand, was inmate 56789/B at the Bountiful Blessed Brides of Jesus Sanatorium.

What patient 56789/B used to be called was anybody's guess. He called himself Hiram F. Doppelganger, and so Hiram it was. In eight months on the case, Jock had made no headway with Hiram, who was convinced that he was a multi-millionaire entrepreneur engaged in daily share transactions on a mobile telephone, when he was actually a man in his declining years wandering around a mental institution with a banana clamped to his left ear.

Hiram continually pestered the nuns to send 'equity details by fax', ordered 'mezzanine funding' with his breakfast, and put up blocks of Gold Coast real estate, breweries and part shares in merchant banks as stakes in his regular poker games with the cleaners. Last week one of the cleaners had won half the Mitsubishi Bank and a golf course in Seattle, although she had accepted three dead matches until the paperwork came through.

Jock had tried everything he could think of. He had delved into possible motives for an invalid pensioner to claim to be a close personal friend of the nation's treasurer. He had pointed out that it was exceedingly unlikely that the nation's treasurer had any close personal friends. He got share listings of companies Hiram claimed to own which showed no trace of him. Hiram would point to a shadowy front company. 'Porkfat Nominees,' he'd say, 'Mate, that's us.'

The Blessed Brides were happy enough that Hiram wasn't violent. Although they disapproved of his Mammon worship, they allowed him his financial magazines from which he gleaned all his jargon of shoddy dealing. He had subscriptions to about twenty of them, from Australia and elsewhere, paid for by a well-meaning alleged nephew who painted nude scenes on expensive guitars for visiting rock stars.

Jock had pointed out articles about broken, debt-ridden high-flyers of the past. He appealed to Hiram's better nature—look what these bastards did to their shareholders! Hiram would not be moved. 'You're right, son,' he'd say, pretending Jock's pencil was a Cuban cigar. 'They got too greedy. I'm not into asset-stripping myself, and I told Warwick about those junk bonds. I warned him.' Jock despaired of such fancies.

He showed Hiram the advertisement in American *Entrepreneur* magazine. 'We have some good reasons why this sign is popping up all over the USA! *Have you seen this missing child?'*. The advertisement carried a photograph of a runaway pre-pubescent child and his description. 'AND WHY THE PEOPLE WHO ARE PUTTING THEM THERE ARE ON THE ROAD TO FINANCIAL SUCCESS. Earn up to $850 a week with minimal cash investment. Affiliation with a National Charitable Missing Child Organisation. Highly Profitable Locations. Be your own BOSS.'

63

Hiram said it was better to get into the Eurobond market in any case. Jock was beginning to worry about Hiram a great deal. His nephew, having run out of good guitar customers with questionable taste, would soon be unable to afford either the magazine subscriptions or the nursing-home fees. And since Hiram was not violent, there was a good chance he'd have to go somewhere else, even though the nuns were fond of him. Jock was worried that Hiram would end up on one of those consumer affairs rip-off programmes. Or at the very least, running some of the television networks on which the programmes appeared. Already, Hiram frequently told Rolf to 'hold all calls from the media'.

Back in his office in Brunswick Street after his latest visit to Hiram, Jock demanded that Vera come across the road to the Funko Bar for a drink. Vera consented, plonked a gorgeous creation of plastic hydrangeas and seagull feathers on her head and took his arm so she didn't get her stilettoes stuck in the tram tracks crossing the road. Once there, she announced loudly that there should be a law against stinging you $6 for a mixed drink. And they didn't have sweet sherry. Jock dropped her off at the flats and went home to write a postcard to Selina. He had chosen a photograph of a woman in a bikini holding a fairy penguin; the colour registration was a bit skewiff: the woman was green, and the penguin mauve. It was perfect.

'Hello there young girlie, get out of it.' Miranda woke Selina with a cup of tea and the morning newspaper. 'Feel like a swim?'

Miranda went for an early swim each day at the Nightcliff pool, a dreamy location on a cliff overlooking the sea, surrounded by lawn and coconut palms. She explained that for the last week the pool had hosted a small band of soldiers who left their weapons on the ground and occasionally went outside the cyclone-wire fence and around to the edge of the cliff to check on their radar systems and guns pointing out to sea.

Sure enough, there they were sitting under a picnic umbrella in khaki. Selina found this extremely disturbing, but Miranda explained it was the follow-up to the annual Operation Frontal military exercise, when the Australian army and its United States advisers pretended they were being attacked by a country going by a code name that didn't sound anything like Indonesia. For seven nights in a row, they could count on being shaken, sometimes literally, by low flying FA 18 Hornets and the deafening roar of B52s thundering overhead. Miranda said she was sure they were also doing a survey on the side for a roof-tiling company. Any trip to the centre of Darwin would produce several lascivious suggestions from visiting soldiers and sailors in the mall. Their revelry was never dampened by the fact that Darwin was always fictitiously bombed into oblivion by the second day of any pretend war.

This was the first year they had run a military exercise in the Build-up, and everyone was terribly grumpy about it.

Back at home for breakfast, Selina read the local paper, full of dubious re-runs from the London *Sun* and from other Australian Murdoch papers, and advertisements for 'night-life'. It was time for the local pub owners to cash in on the influx of lonely soldiers with back pay in their pockets. There was a 'Ladies' Half Yard Sculling Comp' on at the Top End Frontier Hotel, and it had nothing to do with rowing. A Melbourne Bitter special was being held at the Parap Hotel, with low prices on what the locals called 'red cans' (Fosters beer was called blue cans, Carlton, white, and the favourite, Victoria Bitter, was green cans. It was a hangover from droving days, when illiterate itinerants ordered beer by colour.) The standard lunch-time pub fare was advertised heavily: strip and prawn luncheons.

Selina read on. 'Hey, M,' she said, coming upon statistics from a couple of years ago that had just been released. 'Is this for real?' The Northern Territory, with a population approximately the size of a large inner-city suburb of Melbourne or Sydney, had spent seventy-eight million dollars on alcohol in one year. She read out the salient points to Miranda.

'Judging from the activities at the "Rage Bar" just down the road,' said Miranda, 'I'd say it's probably an underestimation.'

Selina turned to the job advertisements. Topless waitress. Nope. Receptionist for a small mining

66

concern. No, thank you. Door-to-door selling. Too hot for that sort of caper. Real-estate agent. She looked shocking in a navy blue lounge suit. Selina was beginning to think that part of her destiny was to spend hours looking in vain at employment pages.

After a cold shower—a pleasure previously unknown to a Melbourne girl—she flounced into the kitchen. Miranda was putting away the milk before it went sour in the heat; just about everything had to go in the fridge to discourage the ants and cockroaches. Last night's dishes were piled up in what Miranda called the 'health hazard corner', so the girls put on a Madonna song, really loud, and did the dishes dance, Selina at the sink and Miranda on putting away detail.

'You could go for that job at the Plaza. My friend Chloe works there—I'm sure she could help. Oh, that reminds me, a couple of her relatives are coming to stay. I'll find out the details today.'

Over a lunch of rock-melon and peanut-butter sangers, they played an old game which had begun with the rash of feminist and psychology books, like *My Mother Myself*, and *Women Who Love Too Much*. 'I'm going to write *Men Who Love Women Who Behave Like Total Weasels*,' began Selina.

'*Women Who Love Men Who Pretend To Love Them Back But Don't Tell Their Wives*,' countered Miranda.

'*My Mother, My God*.'

'*Men Who Love Women Who Love Too Much and Eat At McDonalds*.'

'*I'm OK, You're OK But That Guy Over There is An Alien*.'

'Um, *Women Who Love Men Who Hate James Brown Music*.'

'*Smart Women, Foolish Earrings*.'

'*Emotional Blackmail For Fun and Profit*.'

'*Blondes On Stilts*.'

'Woo. Surrealism. I'm outta here.'

Miranda was off to work a half-afternoon shift, leaving Selina to her job-hunting. They agreed to meet at the Press Club Bar at 6 pm. They push-started the Minx, which seemed to dislike the heat as much as Selina did.

'I can't believe it's ever hotter than this any-where,' she said. 'I'll just go and hose myself down.'

'Dang. And no time to sell tickets,' grizzled Miranda, and headed towards town.

Selina made herself a cup of rose-hip tea and took it out to the verandah with the paper, which was already limp with the humidity. She turned back to the employment page, and circled an ad for a cleaner at the Plaza Hotel with Miranda's eyebrow pencil. She looked at it for a while, thinking of spangly tutus and magic rings, and sighed. Then she thought about Keating the rabbit, and went to get the phone.

Three hours later she was being interviewed on the first floor of the Plaza building, just around the corner from the ABC in the centre of town. It took only about fifteen minutes to circumnav-igate the central business district of Darwin, which basically existed to serve the military, the public service and the tourism industry. Most of the big hotels were usually half empty, subsidised by the government to stay open.

Selina faced the hotel personnel manager, a carefully groomed, middle-aged woman with a hair-do as yeilding as a hard hat, and long, curved, orange fingernails. She asked Selina all the usual questions, and eventually gave her the job, and a locker. Selina confided her frock size for the uniform, a rather bizarre concoction of lemon and pale blue, and learned that she would have six hours work each week day, and every three weeks would have to work the weekend, for which she would receive a less-then-fabulous penalty rate. Still, it was a job, and although the work would be a drag, there was something quasi-glamorous about being able to ferret around other people's rooms when they were out. Who was she kidding? But at least she didn't have to get any flash clothes for work.

She was to front up the following morning, after a call to the Liquor and Allied Trades Union, for an instructional tour by the head of housekeeping service, Miss Krinolopoulous. She bought an ugly postcard of the post-modern (otherwise known as miles of concrete) facade of the Plaza to send to Jock.

The Press Club Bar was only a three-minute walk away. She could sit and wait for Miranda for a while, and read the Plaza instructions to staff. All guests had to be called Sir or Madam, regardless of age, and she would have to wear her hair in a 'neat ponytail or snood'. That sounded highly unlikely, even if she were able to discover the nature of a snood before tomorrow.

The Press Club was already full of ABC reporters,

hacks from the local rag, and several government press secretaries, some of whom were also already full. A couple of them appraised her with bloodshot eyes, but she had learned years ago not to make eye contact with men in bars. She was saved by a young man who introduced himself with, 'You must be Selina. Miranda's held up filing for "PM". I'm Frank McCleary.' He pulled out a seat for her at a table near the bar, and dutifully tried to push through the throng to get her a lime and soda water.

One of the press secretaries, a whippet-thin, bearded man with one arm, lurched up to the table and arshked if he could introdewsh himshelf. He was the presh shecretary for the Minishter for Zoning and hish name was Gavin Bashkerville. Selina knew trouble when she saw it, and nodded politely.

'Whoareyou?' he demanded, leaning forward and breathing Essence of Eighth Green Can at her.

'My name is Selina Plankton. I'm waiting for somebody,' she said, looking past him for Frank, or any other form of rescue.

'Oh, yeah, I know that. Your little girlfriend, ay.' He leered nastily and swayed a little. 'We know what you're up to. We don't approve of that sort of shtuff up here.'

'Excuse me?' said Selina, as Miranda came through the door fanning herself with *Harpers* magazine and made her way over. She reached the table at the same time as Frank. Gavin Baskerville glared at them, and to their collective horror, spat on the floor near Miranda's feet.

'You're a bunch of shocialist bitches,' he slurred.

'The lot of you, Shouthern wankers coming up here and telling ush how to run things. You can't shay all that shit about us. Who do you think you are? You don't matter around here. The ABC ish dead in the water up here. You'll get nothing out of ush.'

He looked from Selina to Miranda. 'Bunch of lezzos. It's shick. You'll get yours.' He was becoming more erratic, and more florid, by the second. He gestured wildly with his glass of beer, sloshing some of it on to Frank's shoes.

'Steady on, mate,' said Frank. Baskerville grabbed him by the tie and pushed him up against the wall. Selina's lime and soda went crashing on to the table and broke into two neat pieces, splashing everywhere.

'You shocialist pricks are finished, I tell you. We don't need you . . . '

Baskerville was dragged away by two of his colleagues, one of whom apologised with a smirk. Miranda glared at him. 'Never smile at a crocodile,' she said. He looked puzzled. She turned to where Baskerville was being calmed with the promise of another beer. 'If you've got a problem with my reporting, Mr Baskerville, take it up with my employer and our lawyers.'

Miranda, Selina and Frank left the bar. Selina was shaking. Frank was patting her on the shoulder. 'Don't worry, it's just the booze talking. He won't even remember it tomorrow. He'll ring up and apologise to Fingle, and everyone will forget about it. Being rat-faced pissed is an all-purpose excuse up here.'

'I hate this place,' brooded Miranda. 'No, I don't, I mean, I hate the fact that those crocodiles run it. The government and the mining companies and the old-timer public servants who wouldn't know independence if it bit them on the bum. Profit-driven, amoral, plundering, wall-eyed, greedy, complacent old blokes with hardened arteries and bat-shit where their souls should be. I hate them. They're mostly well-paid liars and corrupt old drunks. It's like they've been bred for it. They tell the tourists that crocs have evolved over millions of years into the perfect killing machine. Those bastards have developed over millions of long lunches into the perfect born-to-rule machines. The Crocodile Club. A protected species.'

'For God's sake, M,' said Selina. 'Get off your high horse and start protecting yourself. What are you going to do? You can't live with this sort of stuff happening to you all the time.'

'I'm going to wait until I get a big story that will bury the lot of them, and then I'm getting out. I can play rough, too. I'm just going to do it with the truth.'

'Oh gawd,' sighed Frank. 'You know perfectly well we've thrown scandal after scandal at them and they keep winning elections. Look how long Bjelke-Petersen held on in Queensland. Franklin got caught for saying "coons" for God's sake, and he didn't resign. You can't run a vendetta, Miranda, your job is to report the facts.'

'Don't lecture me about ethics, Frank. I'm not going to lie, I'm just going to do some more digging. There must be something we can find. They can't have the whole place sewn up. There must be a public servant with dirt who isn't afraid to dish it.'

'Well shut up about it then, or it'll just get worse for you,' said Frank. 'Can you drop me off at Parap on your way home?'

Miranda and Selina drove most of the way home in silence. 'Sellie, have you kept up the self-defence practice?'

'Yeah. You?'

'Yeah. I think we might need it.'

'Oh per-lease, M, don't you think this is getting a little bit out of proportion? Just let things go quiet for a while, like Frank said. They'll have a new target in a minute. Then hit them with something big.'

'I suppose you're right,' said Miranda, as she parked the Minx a short walk from the curb and they got out.

Selina put her arm around her friend. 'Guess what? I got a job. I start tomorrow, cleaning rooms at the Plaza.'

Miranda smiled. 'And hacking their computer records.'

'Do you want a cup of tea or should I fill the bath with ice-cubes?'

'Tea, please.'

'You've acclimatised.'

'No I haven't. I still think I can bring down the government by Friday.'

5

Suite Talk

Hiram F. Doppelganger was explaining to a nun the infinitesimal difference between playing the stock-market and playing roulette on mescalin when Jock arrived on his usual humour-the-patient rounds. Rolf and Sister Mary-Louise (known as Boom-Boom to her friends) went off to see what they could find in the way of dilapidated tennis balls perfumed with Blood and Bone fertiliser.

'Have you heard, boy?' boomed Hiram, wiggling his thermometer like Groucho Marx with a cigar, 'I'm going up in the world! Expansion plans! What do you say; let's corner the market on this lithium stuff.'

'Hiram,' sighed Jock. 'As sure as I'm a Serbo-

Scottish lunatic, you're not fit for the streets of this fair-to-middling city. Still, neither am I, and I haven't been locked up yet.'

'Locked up!?' boomed Hiram. 'Not on your nelly! We'll strip their assets! No one will have a monopoly on lithium but us! Have faith, my boy! Get an eyeful of the prospectus!' He handed Jock a pamphlet on the Incontinence Association of Australia. 'I give great meeting!'

'I hear you're going to live with your nephew,' tried Jock.

'Nope. Little entrepreneur is off to work with some royalty. Something about guitars, Minneapolis and a Prince chap. I'm on my own. Well, I'm prepared to start from the bottom again,' said Hiram.

'Oh God, I need a holiday,' said Jock.

'Just the ticket! Where are we going, laddie? Get my secretary to make the arrangements. Got the company credit card? Let's kick serious arse! We'll blow out the all ordinaries index! Get me my banana!'

'Oh God,' said Jock.

Darwin, Tuesday 15 December 1998

As it happened, Selina did not spend her first hours at the Plaza hacking into the computer system or making block bookings for the Central Intelligence Ball in Langley, Virginia, both of Miranda's

75

suggestions being declined with a smirk. Besides, she was far too busy cleaning windows, doing hospital corners on the bed-linen, remembering not to use the guest lifts, going downstairs for more supplies of soap, shampoo, shower caps and everything else the guests nicked.

She had bagged her own trolley, which had a mirror polish spray and a surface polish spray and towels and other supplies, but also an airmail copy of *Spin* magazine with a Sinead O'Connor interview she'd pinched from Miranda, and a set of antennae Selina had bought at the Royal Melbourne Show on the same day that she kissed her first boy behind the wood-chopping pavilion. His name was Ern and he was better at the Under Sixteen Underhand than kissing. Selina wore the antennae while cleaning empty rooms, and occasionally attempted a spirited polka between bathroom and balcony.

She had only been sprung once, by a Japanese couple, who made absolutely no mention of it, either to Selina, or, happily, to management. Selina learned quickly: even flash hotels used torn and worn sheets; cleaning up a honeymoon suite was murder, mainly because of the confetti, women were, in general, about forty times messier than men and flight attendants were the pits when it came to untidiness; Japanese couples usually asked for twin beds, slept in one bed, and rumpled the other insufficiently to fool a housemaid.

Selina had made friends immediately with Miranda's friend Chloe Futura, the daytime receptionist. At morning tea, Selina told her the Jock story, and Chloe had an endless supply of stories about her large collection of relatives and friends.

Miranda had already told her how Chloe's husband had died of apoplexy the previous year. He had accidentally read the Macquarie Dictionary definition of 'furburger', and died in hysterics, tears rolling down his cheeks, clutching a Big Whopper. Chloe hadn't been able to finish a crossword since.

Chloe dedicated herself to other people's kids as well as her own mob of eight and was known as 'Aunty' to a lot of people who were not blood relatives. Three successive managers of the Plaza, sent to 'see what they could do' with Darwin after management courses, had tried to shift Chloe from the front desk on the grounds that she was 'not quite right for the Plaza image'. All were thwarted by the unprecedented number of letters to the management about her courteous service.

More than once she covered a complaint about Selina on her first morning, sending her scurrying to replace a towel or stationery. And she had promised to teach Selina how to use the front desk computer, so that she'd have a better chance of being a stand-in receptionist. In return, Selina was going to present herself at Chloe's second granddaughter's eighth birthday and do some magic.

Selina would go almost anywhere that had air-conditioning. Only three days in and she was already finding the Build-up pretty hard to take. Oh, it wasn't the fact that she had developed heat rashes in parts of her body she didn't even know she had. And it wasn't that at night it got so hot and humid she dreamed that her brain was melting and flowing on to the pillow. It wasn't that she couldn't muster the energy for much more than lying on the verandah and reading magazines. It wasn't that almost everyone around her seemed to behave like they had the worst pre-menstrual tension known to humankind (especially the men). It wasn't that beer was omnipresent, and she hated beer. It wasn't that she was getting used to the feel of sweat sliding down her back and from under her breasts.

No, it was just the Build-up. The sense that something was about to happen. Clouds gathered in the afternoon, full of portent but devoid of rain. What, in Melbourne, would have produced proper raindrops and lots of them, just melted into more heat, more humidity, more edge-of-madness waiting. It made Selina think of the only piece of information she had ever retained from science class at Manangatang High. It was the opposite of kinetic energy; potential energy? Was that it? Like a cat on its haunches ready to spring, or those old-fashioned posters of strapping Soviet lads, stripped to the waist near a sheaf of wheat and staring in a Marxist sort of a way into the distance.

Selina was already beginning to think she wasn't going to get through the Build-up with her sanity intact. Out of the air-conditioning, she felt soggy most of the time. She couldn't go for a swim in the sea for fear of deadly jellyfish or crocodiles, and she missed a beach you could get yourself into. She had been meaning to ask Miranda why people chose to live through the Build-up if they weren't born here, but Miranda didn't seem to mind oppression, as long as it was climatic and not political. It was her stolid contention that by Christmas it would be raining like crazy for weeks on end. Strangely enough, Selina did not find this comforting.

As Selina polkaed her way across room 1417, Miranda was sitting down in the government offices, face to face with her chosen enemy, Harold Franklin OBE (services to pissing in the right pockets), former policeman, Deputy Premier, Minister for Zoning, Police and Meteorological Services.

Miranda was in her dress-for-striking terror-into-the-interviewee outfit, a light black linen suit with white silk shirt and shoes with one-inch heels. The Minister hauled almost all of himself out of the chair to shake her cool hand, and flopped back down, dislodging several pieces of plaster from the ceiling underneath, which fell on to the desk of an accounts clerk in the tourism office. The clerk, inured, brushed the excess plaster from his triplicate form requesting a new desk.

'Miranda,' said the Minister, who was flanked by piles of documents and Gavin Baskerville.

'Minister,' said Miranda, and began setting up her standard-issue ABC tape recorder. 'It won't lead the bulletin, but let's get down to the new zoning law amendments.'

'Sure,' said Franklin. 'Is that thing on yet?'

'Nearly,' said Miranda, looping a piece of tape around the second reel.

'Great tits,' said Mr Baskerville, from the corner.

Miranda hit the start button viciously and stared at him with her chin high.

'Testy, testy,' said the Minister into the microphone. Miranda felt murderous.

Across town, Selina was taking the sheets off a double bed in the deluxo suite when something caught her eye. Under one of the pillows was an empty Polly Waffle packet, and under the other was the remains of the Polly Waffle itself, with the chocolate coating nibbled away in a spiral pattern. Only one man could be responsible for this act of grossness. She'd told him that Polly Waffles were made by the same company that flogged dubious baby food formulas to the Third World, but Briian the Crazed Architect was no boycotter. Selina picked up the phone next to the bed and punched the number for reception, her scalp tingling.

'Chloe? Selina. I'm in 1418. Who's the inmate?'

'Not your type,' said Chloe from the front desk on the ground floor, as she smiled encouragingly at a Japanese tourist filling out his registration form in German.

'You said it. Dirt?'

Chloe tapped at the computer with one hand, waited for the green letters to flash up on the screen, then, 'Briian Bodoni. Firm of Mega Concrete Hype Inc. Open-ended booking, um . . . paying by American Express gold card. Half-emptied the mini-bar his first night here . . . ah . . . let's see, currently somewhere over Kakadu on the Scenic Air run. What's wrong, hon, find a body or something?'

'No, Chloe, just a mangled Polly Waffle.'

'Uh-huh. Need the house detective?'

'I'll get back to you, smart-arse. Thanks,' said Selina.

'Any time.' Chloe hung up, and turned a dazzling smile of welcome on Mr Harasato, handed him the key and tried 'Arigato' in a German accent.

In 1418, Selina sat down on the bed, after a quick reconnaissance to make sure it was otherwise free of molested chocolate bars. Scenic Air wouldn't deliver its load of tourists back to the hotel until 3 pm. She had an hour: plenty of time for a little snooping.

It seemed that Briian had a new job. There were four polyester safari suits lined up in the mirrored wardrobe, each more expensive than the last, and five pairs of white shoes, the type favoured by property developers and patronising gynaecologists. 'Euww,' said Selina. She had found the socks.

She picked the combination lock on his briefcase in six minutes, and opened it gingerly. There was a stack of business cards which announced, 'Development and Planning Consultant' in beige on white. 'I suppose "Crazed Architect" doesn't have quite the right ring to it,' Selina thought. Later, she would try to regret looking into the briefcase, but it's useless to try to regret something. Either you do, or you don't.

Remembering the position of each item, Selina removed a roll of plans, two documents, and looked carefully at the contents of Briian's briefcase, then she had to sit down. She forgot to check for chocolate.

Briian was up to his neck in what developers

call a resort complex, when they don't want people to think about concrete. Only this wasn't any old resort complex. The list of features in the fattest document read: thirty-five-storey hotel complex, casino, marina with forty-seven major berths and fifty-three pleasure craft, car-park, 'up-market strip function room' and conference centre.

And it was going to be built opposite Miranda's house.

She unrolled the plans carefully, using a pair of Briian's white shoes to hold down the corners. She tried to think what the architect's impression of the finished building reminded her of—it looked like the aliens had landed on a thirty-five-storey concrete matchbox.

Selina took the plans and documents to the conference centre on the first floor and photocopied everything she could in half an hour. Back in Briian's room, she replaced everything as she found it, and then short-sheeted the bed. Resisting the impulse to wipe her fingerprints off the room, she scooped the chocolate-bar wrapper into the rubbish bag and wheeled her trolley purposefully out of room 1418, feather dusters swaying jauntily. Then she went downstairs to resign. Chloe suggested that she ought to seek professional help about her obsession with mauled confectionery, which made Selina think of Jock.

At that moment, Jock was winding up an interview with a prospective patient. Her family wanted to have the old woman committed, but Jock was forming the opinion that she would be better off in a good nursing home than a mental institution.

He was supposed to be doing an assessment, but in fact he was sitting in an enormous, over-stuffed armchair in a room chock-a-block with valuable antiques. Across from him, an eighty-nine-year-old woman was perched on a stool, wearing aviator goggles, a pink satin dressing-gown and silver sandals with a tiny, framed picture of Amy Johnson on each toe.

'So, Mrs M,' said Jock, putting down a fine bone-china cup and saucer with lime flavoured fizzy drink in it. 'Why *did* you sew all of your other crockery into the curtains?'

'So that nobody could steal it, of course,' she said in a strong voice.

'Correct. And the lamingtons on the lounge-room floor?'

'For attracting rats,' she smiled patronisingly.

'That should certainly do it, Mrs M.'

'Yes, young man. Another savoury, perhaps?' She proffered a plate.

'No thank you, I'm off jam and cardboard just at the moment,' he said politely.

'It's the war, dear.'

'I shouldn't be at all surprised. Until Thursday, then?'

'Delighted.'

'Me too.'

Mrs M showed Jock the window. He thoughtfully moved the Ming vase on the sill before climbing out. Mrs M gave him a big wave from the mansion as he did a few wheelies around the circular gravel driveway ringed with poppies and ranunculi. No wonder the family wanted power of attorney.

'*Rattus rattus,*' said Mrs M to herself, as she went to the kitchen for some more lamingtons.

'Oh God,' said Jock to himself as he drove down Punt Road. 'I need a holiday. I think I'll ring Selina tonight. At least she doesn't want to move in with me. Or eat cardboard. That's my kinda woman.'

Darwin, later that day

Selina and Miranda were doing a good impression of languid on the balcony that evening. Miranda had demanded to tell her news first.

'And then, our esteemed Minister of the Crown waited until the recorder was packed up, and said "All you need is a good fuck!"'

Selina choked on her cordial. 'Noooo. Who did he suggest? Was he going to hire somebody?'

Miranda giggled. 'Do you know, I really believe he thought he could manage it himself.'

'What on earth did you say?' Selina asked, wiping away tears.

'I told the old stoat that I had known since I was fourteen that I was a lesbian, and it was men

84

like him that constantly reinforced my decision.'

'You didn't!'

'When in doubt, hit 'em with the truth,' said Miranda. 'All that, just for a pathetic thirty-second story on changes to the zoning regulations. *Quelle* boredom! I'm sure there's something dastardly about this, but I can't put my finger on it. Or, maybe I'm just getting cynical. Even the crocodiles have to tinker with the odd bit of legislation I suppose. Oh, I forgot to tell you, Chloe's relatives *are* coming to stay tomorrow, and there might be twenty of them.'

'Wait, my turn,' said Selina. 'Check this out.' She reached into her voluminous hat-box cum handbag, and produced the plans she had found in Briian's room.

Miranda looked through them, biting her lip, for three minutes. 'Bingo,' she breathed.

'What? What?' Selina said.

'Well, this explains a lot,' said Miranda. 'Franklin's what you might call implicated. See the proposal to get hold of the land? It's owned by Franklin's family company. Franklin said today they're going to rezone this piece of foreshore from public use to multi-use. He said it was so they could build an Aboriginal cultural centre. Sure. I thought he was throwing out a crumb, because there's no chance of the local Aborigines getting this land back. Since Statehood, all land claims have been disallowed. Snaky; once it's zoned multi-use, you see, he's allowed to sell it. The development company buys it, and *quelle surprise*, the government says it's too big a chance to resist.

Jobs, tourism, boom times ahead for the Territory. Oh, yeah, I can see it now. Selina, this is fantastic. This is what I've been waiting for. I'll sink him with this.' Miranda seemed to come out of a trance. 'Where did you get it?'

Selina began to explain, just as a white Commodore pulled into the foreshore car-park across the road, and two men got out of it.

'Hey,' said Miranda. 'That's the same two guys who were sitting there when I rang you in Melbourne. Maybe they weren't looking at me at all—perhaps they had something to do with this thing,' she tapped the plans.

The two men, heavy-set and grim, were walking across the road towards the house. Another car pulled up, and Briian Bodoni got out. He looked up, framed from behind by another fabulous sunset he didn't even glance at. 'That's her!' he shouted. The two men began to run through the pawpaw trees on the front lawn towards the stairs.

'They're looking for you now!' shouted Selina, as she ran to the phone.

There was no time.

6

Violent Crumble

As the first Ministerial wide-boy crashed through the door, and before he could say anything at all, he was felled with one end of a didjiridu. Miranda was still standing on the chair next to the door holding the other end of the didjiridu when she heard the screeching of car brakes at the front of the house. More of them!

Thug Number One lay on the floor looking rather surprised, as well he might, for he had just been struck nearly senseless by a young woman in a pink sarong.

As the second member of the thug brigade came through the door, Selina, still trying to dial with one hand, tripped him up with the mop and he sprawled across the floor, sliding some distance on a pandanus mat. Unfortunately he had grabbed

Miranda's left ankle on the way past, and dragged her off the chair.

Briian was the next through the door, propelled by three more large packages of feral testosterone who must have arrived in the latest car. Even through her fear, Selina reckoned that there would shortly be enough people for an impromptu game of touch footy in the lounge-room.

She had enough time to bite one of the thugs on the ear, head-butt another and address some serious attention to Briian's more tender parts before the smallest of the thugs with the scariest eyes pinned her arms behind her. She broke away with deft use of the backwards shin-scrape, but by this time the bite victim settled matters momentarily with the arresting production of a revolver. Selina sat on the nearest chair.

Miranda had lost consciousness when she hit the floor, and was just coming around. All the people in the room except Miranda were breathing heavily, from exertion or, in Briian's case, anger. As a result of Selina's displeasure in being manhandled, and her expression of same, several pictures had been knocked off the wall and two chairs were looking remarkably like firewood.

'Lie still, M,' said Selina. She looked around the room, and then she looked at Briian. Well not really at him, kind of through him, and then at the man with the gun.

'May I help you?' she asked.

'Cute,' he said. 'Sit there and shut up.' He turned to Miranda's victim, who was sitting on her in the middle of the floor. 'For Gawd's sake, Ken, this was meant to be easy. No rough stuff, remember? They're just a coupla girls. Same goes for you two,' he said to Selina's victims, who were looking rather sheepish. 'She's only five foot two.'

'Five foot four, Lefty,' said Selina.

'Shut up. Who are you calling Lefty, anyway? Never mind. Briian, make yourself useful and find those plans. Ken, tie up the blonde.'

Miranda, who was surely the last woman in the world to get a big kick out of being called 'the blonde', got up from the floor slowly.

'OK,' said Ken, 'Come over here and sit in the chair and I'll . . . Aaaarrrgghhhh!' Miranda had punched him on the nose and he was bleeding all down the front of his nice navy suit and red tie, although it didn't show up so badly on the tie as on the white shirt. It was a good score from Miranda, but it did make Ken forget any of the more gentlemanly portions of himself and he slugged her right back.

Miranda fell heavily on the floor, unconscious again. Selina shouted, and was pushed back into her chair. She began to cry. The man with the gun seemed pleased to see this, and concluded that it was a sign of weakness rather than a sign of being rather upset.

'Ay, ay, ay, steady on,' said the gunman, as the man with the blood nose prepared to hit Miranda again. 'Jesus. Sit down, you lot,' he said to his colleagues, 'I've got to work this out. I don't know what to do with the sheilas.'

Selina then said a few things that she had heard in the shearing shed, and once repeated in the kitchen when she was very small. It had led to a marathon lecture from Dot, although Len had copped the worst of it when he came home for tea, for allowing his daughter to hear such words.

Briian came in off the verandah with the photocopies of the plans rolled up in one hand. He hadn't even mussed up his white safari suit. He sneered at Selina.

'Leave it to Billy Idol,' Selina said. 'You bastard, Briian, if I could get my hands on you I'd rip your testicles off and shove them in your side pockets!'

Briian looked affronted. Everyone else looked speculatively at his pockets.

Then the telephone rang. It was such a normal sound in such an absurd situation.

'It's Miranda's work. If I don't answer it they'll think something's wrong,' said Selina quickly. 'Let me answer.'

'No way, smarty pants,' said Lefty. He gestured with the gun. 'Briian—pick it up and fix it. She'll be trouble.'

'Leave it to me,' said the Crazed Architect, and swaggered over to the phone.

Beep Beep Blibeep Beep.

'Hello?'

'Hello, who's that?'

'I asked you first, turkey.'

'No you didn't, you just said hello. Could I speak to Selina please?'

'What do you want? She's not here.'

'It's Jock Jovanovich. You sound familiar . . . '

Selina screamed, and one of the thugs clamped

his hand over her mouth. She promptly bit it and he screamed, too.

'What's going on?' demanded Jock, alarmed, and a very long way away.

'Just having a little party,' said Briian. 'I'm her *boy*friend. Everything's fine.'

'Wait a minute,' said Jock. 'You're the Crazed Architect! What are you doing there? She wouldn't touch you for quids!'

'She would so!' remonstrated Briian's ego, and therefore his mouth. 'She's crazy-mad in love with me. Now bugger off!'

As Briian hung up, Selina screamed again, amid renewed scuffling.

Briian turned to the gunman and smiled. 'Completely foxed him,' he said.

The gunman sighed and unplugged the phone. 'I think we'd better get out of here.'

Wednesday 16 December 1998

When the morning paper hit the front lawn, Miranda was still unconscious. She woke to the sounds of birds and a fierce argument next door which appeared to have something to do with the absence of breakfast cereal. It was the sort of argument likely to lead to violent mayhem in the prevailing weather conditions, but there was no time to think about that now.

Miranda lay on the floor and looked at the ceiling

fan for a while. She got to her feet slowly and felt her jaw, and then the back of her head, which caused her to say 'ouch' twice. She was still feeling a little dizzy and deranged, but nothing a journalist who ever had a drink doesn't know about, so she went downstairs to get the paper.

'I wonder what I was drinking,' she thought to herself on the way down the slightly rickety stairs to the garden. Even the early morning sun was too bright, and she stopped halfway down the stairs, squinting to see where the newspaper had landed. Oh, great. Right in the middle of the bougainvillea again. She dug it out with the rusty fishing rod reserved for this purpose, and checked out the headline.

FRANKLIN GOLF PLAN NT BOON, she read. After giving Miranda a dull interview on legislative details, Harold Franklin had seen fit to give the *Territory Voice* an exclusive insight into his plans to rezone his foreshore land to 'multi-use' so that public mini-golf links could be built to attract tourists and locals alike.

Miranda stood on the front lawn in a golden haze and a pink sarong, staring at the headline. 'That snake-eyed rat-legged tattooed custard-fondler,' she said. 'I know what he's up to! He's trying to . . . '

She was interrupted by the arrival of a large, dusty van, and a Mini Moke on the nature strip. She gazed through the trees, with not much going on in her brain, as Chloe got out of the Mini Moke and started bashing at the door of the van with a stout piece of wood. After a few convincing blows,

92

and much shouting from the inside of the van, she gave up.

Miranda unlatched the gate and stepped out on to the driveway. 'What are you doing here, Chloe?'

'Eh?' said Chloe, who was walking around the van trying to open the dust-caked windows. 'I told you yesterday my mob was coming up from Nyampuju, don't you remember? It's the dancing rock mob, they've got a couple of gigs in town this week. You said it was all right for them to stay here, and that you'd fix it with Sellie last night.'

By this time Chloe was trying the far windows. 'They were going to stay at Town Reserve, but they want a proper women's camp, no blokes or drunks around. You know how it is . . . All right ladies,' Chloe was now addressing the van itself. 'It's proper job stuck, that door now. You mob kick and knock im out. We'll get that land council mob to fix it by and by.'

A chorus of 'Yuwayi' came from the truck and then there was a mighty big noise as the door came off its hinge and fell into the gutter.

'Hello ladies!' shouted Chloe happily. 'Hello Aunty, hello Sister, hello Mummy, hello you Mummy there, and Granny . . . this is Miranda, you can camp here, no worries, no grog.' Chloe finally looked around at Miranda, who was transfixed with horror, staring at the open door of the van.

Still more women with beautiful brown eyes and dark skin were piling out, carrying babies, rolled up swags, small children, rolled up pieces of canvas, billy cans, plastic bags, battered guitars, a high-hat cymbal set and blankets. All the women were dressed in dusty, sleeveless frocks, and were barefoot. They smiled shyly at Miranda.

'Hey,' said Chloe. 'They've been on the road for fifteen hours with a stuck door. They're bound to look a bit the worse for wear. Just point us in the direction of the washing machine and the shower, love, and I'll give Sellie a lift to work. Bogey for you mob, ay, Ivy.'

'Yuwayi, Sister, a shower, that's right,' said a sprightly-looking teenager. 'This one here think we're a mob of dirty blackfellas, eh?' she grinned.

'No, don't be silly,' said Miranda, in a daze. 'It's just the door. The door, the door . . . Smashing, smashing. Can't remember . . . Franklin. I know what he did. He gave them the scoop. I know what he did. I know . . . ' she trailed off.

The teenage girl briefly spoke in language, and a guarded look came over the faces of the visitors. They continued to smile shyly, and held tightly to the children.

If there's one thing Aborigines are used to, it's being polite to strangely disjointed white people, although Miranda worked for a different arm of government from the usual lot.

'No, not myall, this one,' said Chloe. 'She's sick, I think.' Chloe put her hand up to Miranda's face, and looked her straight in the eye. She pushed her hair back from her forehead and saw a deep welt, then she noticed the bruise on Miranda's jaw.

'No good,' said an elderly woman.

'No good, Aunty. Let's get her inside.' Chloe led Miranda by the hand up the stairs, and stopped at the splintered door. Her mouth dropped open.

'You see?' said Miranda. 'It's all right, Chloe, I was just trying to remember to get the door fixed. Come on in, ladies, it's a bit of a mess, but we'll fix 'im up for you mob.'

The women came in, hushed now, looking at Chloe. Something terrible had happened here. There was blood on the floor, and so many things were broken. Two older ladies pushed through the crowd, making a high, wailing sound.

'Where's Sellie?' Chloe said, grasping Miranda's hand tightly and looking into her pale face.

'Oh, she lives in Melbourne,' Miranda said airily.

'Oh no,' said Chloe, surveying the room. 'You got to snap out of this girl, she's in trouble.' Chloe looked at the bedraggled arrangement of women in the doorway. 'You mob put the swags, and everything in the bedrooms. Leave 'im this one first.' Chloe turned to the four teenage girls who were standing together, looking in distaste at the blood. 'You help your aunties there. And put that billy on the stove, this one needs tee-lip now,' she added.

'Oh yes, a cup of tea, what a lovely idea,' said Miranda. The girls looked at each other.

'Warrungka,' said one of them significantly.

'Warrungka,' said Miranda dreamily, hugging the *Territory Voice* to her chest. 'Is that my Aboriginal tribal name?'

'No, it means soft in the head,' said Chloe. 'Sit down while I ring my old friend the Police Commissioner.'

'Oh', said Miranda.

Chloe plugged in the phone, consulted the Plaza

95

notebook in her handbag, dialled, and began to talk over a background of chatter and symphonic water noises—boiling on the stove, running in the shower, and slooshing in the washing machine downstairs.

Within fifteen minutes, five constables, a doctor, two sergeants and Police Commissioner Mick Maguire were trying to find a piece of door they could knock on. All of Chloe's relatives skittered into various hidey-holes around the house until she assured them that the police were looking for bad men.

The constables set about tagging things and measuring things and taking photographs in the lounge-room, and recording the skid marks on the road outside. The doctor attended to Miranda, shining a little torch in her eyes, holding up various fingers and getting the wrong answers when he asked how many there were. Then he asked the name of the current prime minister. The doctor had heard many different answers to this, among them Ron Barassi and Prince Charles, but never had a severely concussed interviewee reeled off all the names of the recently re-shuffled Federal Cabinet and their responsibilities.

At this, the doctor announced that he was taking Miranda to the hospital for observation. Obviously she was a cactus witness as far as any mayhem went because she couldn't remember anything except the Cabinet, and she ought to be closely watched.

The Police Commissioner, who had grown up with Chloe in the house and regarded her as not only the best story-teller ever, but the finest scone maker in the Darwin district, had further discussions with Chloe in the laundry.

'Chloe, there's not much I can do. I can get everyone to look out for your friend, and I can have a chat to the manager of the hotel to find out why she resigned yesterday. But short of any further evidence, I'm stumped. We don't know of any sus characters in town, but we've dusted the joint—sorry, lounge-room—for prints and we'll see what we come up with, OK? I'll do my best.'

Chloe trusted Mick Maguire, and well she might; she had 'grown him up' as nanny and housekeeper, and taught him most of his morals. She flew into a temper when anybody in her hearing talked about police corruption as a general problem. 'There are bent coppers and there are good coppers,' she would say. 'And make sure you don't get them mixed up.'

She told Mick that Miranda had been afraid to call the police once before because she thought Harold Franklin was behind plans to rough her up. 'If Franklin ever tried to stick his oar in I'd have him for brekky,' Maguire replied. 'Which is not to say that he's not very handy when we want someone to squawk about more police powers.'

'You've got quite enough already,' said Chloe, in the same way she used to speak of his cake consumption. 'I'll ring you this afternoon and see how you're getting on.'

'Just standard procedure, Chloe,' said Maguire, on his way out.

'Yeah, and the Police Commissioner attends every house call, too, ay,' she retorted.

An elderly woman came out of the cupboard in the hall next to the kitchen.

'What are you doing in there, Nungarrayi?' asked Chloe.

'Well, I just think more better be inside quiet time when police mob around,' said the old woman, who was speaking in the seventh language she had learned—Kriol, a Territory mix of English and Aboriginal languages. 'They say killing stop this time now, modern day, whitefella law, but might be.'

She spoke in language for a while, about her mother's country.

'Yes,' said Chloe quietly, holding the woman's hand. 'I'm going to work now, Aunty. You can do that painting for exhibition about your mother's country, that river story. You keep them young girls all right, and I'll come around lunchtime with bread, and tomato, and corned beef, everything. All right? You safe here. Give that Ivy, that singing one this telephone number. She can ring that telephone if you want me here. You savvy?'

'Yuwayi daughter. Boh-Boh.'

'Boh-Boh, Aunty.'

Selina, at that moment, was finding out just how bad the Build-up could be when you are trussed up in the boot of a late-model Commodore. She had managed to untie herself with fairly rudimentary magic knowledge, but there still wasn't a lot of room to practise the tango in. She tried to think straight, make a plan, but it was so hot, and she had to concentrate on not banging against the sides of the boot too much, or hitting her head on one of her hat-boxes, which she had insisted on bringing with her.

'Lefty', as she now called him, had checked it for hidden weapons, and found only clothes, hairpins, a diary, fluff, postcard, Crowded House tape, tampons, pair of gold lurex gloves, some pens and soap. It had not occurred to him to check for a hidden compartment. Selina was trying to remember what was in the secret compartment, but she was also very tired. She had tried to stay awake all night to work out where the thug brigade was taking her.

At the first stop, she calculated that she was at a big house overlooking Fannie Bay and the yacht club. She heard Franklin's voice and an argument. They had bundled her back into the boot, taken her to another house and left her tied up and blindfolded in a room for a few hours. Now they were on the road again. As Selina braced herself against another swerve, she thought about Miranda, and prayed to every god she had ever heard of that her friend would be all right.

Then she thought of Jock. It must have been him on the phone. Had he twigged that there was something wrong? Would the cops care, or were they all in Franklin's pocket? Were they going to kill her? Would she get breakfast? Could she stand much more of this heat? She broke into a short, unexpected, maniacal laugh, something usually associated only with her love life.

The car stopped, she heard doors slam, and

voices. The boot was opened. 'Get her on to the boat, Ken,' she heard.

'Perhaps I'm going on a cruise,' Selina thought. She felt the sun strike her face with full force and shivered.

As Chloe arrived back at Miranda's with the lunch, a taxi pulled up. Chloe, mindful of keeping a watchful eye on proceedings, stood on the lowest stair and looked through the fence. A man got out wearing a frightful orange Hawaiian shirt that was not so much loud as unto nine brass bands playing 'Girl from Ipanema'; he was followed by a blue heeler with a red, yellow and black collar, and an older, stout man in a beige safari suit wearing a baseball cap with 'Forbes' embroidered on the crown. They had a few pieces of luggage: a green roll-bag, two briefcases, a dog's bowl, a balding tennis ball which smelled bloody awful and a tiny suitcase that looked like a child's lunch box.

'Oh great,' breathed Chloe. 'Warrungka City.'

The three arrivals came in the gate and closed it behind them.

'Pleased to meet you, madam,' announced Hiram, sweeping off his baseball cap. 'Hiram F. Doppelganger at your service. Take-overs, asset-stripping, deals on wheels.'

'G'day,' said Chloe. She looked to Jock. 'Can you do any better than that?'

'G'day,' he said. 'I'm Jock Jovanovich. Serbo-Scottish southern psychiatrist. Friend of Selina's. Worried about her. My blue heeler, Rolf. Called late last night. Bloke answered the phone, heard Selina scream in the background. Think bloke was Briian Bodoni, Crazed Architect. Said he was Sellie's boyfriend. Unlikely. Needed holiday. Got plane this morning. Had to bring patient. Hiram. Is Selina OK?'

Chloe shook her head. 'I don't think so. We don't know where she is. Miranda's been knocked out, and she's in the hospital. But the cops don't have any leads, and it sounds like you've got one. I knew he wasn't her type. You'd better come in. Jock, is it? Is this other fella dangerous?'

'No,' said Jock. 'Just crazy.'

Rolf licked her ankle.

On the way up the stairs, Chloe half turned and said, 'I don't reckon you're going to have much of a holiday, sport. We've got to find that girl.'

'Looks like it,' said Jock, hoping he sounded terribly gruff and knowledgeable, and actually feeling very hot, freaked out, sweaty, and pretty much incapable of clarity in the thoughts department. 'Is it always this hot?'

'No.'

'Good.'

'Sometimes it's hotter.'

'Oh, beaut.'

The blood on the lounge-room floor had been cleaned up, but many of the broken things remained scattered around. The door was still just bits of splintered timber.

'Looks like she's a fighter, that Sellie,' nodded Chloe. 'How come you know her?'

'She was kind of a patient. A friend. I gave her some money to get away from Briian—the bloke on the phone. I don't understand what he's doing here . . . God, look at this place.'

'Oh, you're the one. Yeah, she likes you.'

'Shouldn't we call the police?' asked Jock.

'No, I was just going to suggest we play Skippy,' said Chloe, her hand already on the phone.

This time a young constable came to take Jock's statement. Jock could fix a rough time for the scream, and said that he was pretty sure the voice was Briian's. Chloe rang the Plaza to find that the Crazed Architect was in his room.

Within an hour, Mick Maguire had called her back to say that Briian denied being at Selina's the night before. He denied even knowing that she was in Darwin. They could have pulled him in for some further questioning but his alibi was a meeting with Minister Franklin about some plans for a mini-golf course in Tennant Creek, and it was unshakeable. Franklin had confirmed it, and also given an impromptu character reference.

By this time, Rolf had gone to sleep and was having his tail painted by one of the children, all of whom had been threatened with spiritual and physical punishments if they ventured anywhere near the road. Some of the women had laid out half-finished paintings on the verandah, and were patiently dot-dotting with the ends of twigs. They talked about the stories they were painting, and gossiped about the people back home and the strange goings-on in this whitefella house.

Hiram was chatting to an old woman about foreign exchange futures. She was ignoring him, but he didn't seem to mind.

Chloe and Jock sat at the lounge-room table under the ceiling fan, their hair ruffling slightly. Jock was polishing off the last piece of rock-melon, and peeling an orange for one of the smaller children, who was sitting on his knee, tracing the pictures on his shirt with his tiny index finger.

'Well, Chloe,' Jock was saying, 'I don't know where we go from here. We're not going to get very far calling the Minister an out-and-out lying-mongrel-dog-bastard-weasel-dick-mother- . . . '

'No,' Chloe interrupted, pointing to the kids. 'Miranda can't remember anything, and sitting around here isn't helping to get Selina back. We don't even know if she's alive or dead.'

Jock looked at Chloe, and said, 'She's alive.'

'Yeah, I think she is, too. But what do we do now? We've gone as far as we can with the coppers.'

'Yes, your mate Mick sounds all right. I don't know. I suppose the best place to start is with this Franklin character. I can't see how he could be involved with violence and kidnapping, but that was definitely Briian on the phone, and Franklin's covering for him, so he must be involved. I s'pose I'll go and see him. Can I leave Hiram with you?'

'Nope,' said Chloe. 'I've got to go back to work. And none of you can stay here. This is a women's camp. These are my relatives, from an outstation near Nyampuju, down in desert country. The young girls—the teenagers—are in a band called

103

Women's Business. Their mothers and aunties and grannies are chaperones . . . dancers and artists too. They're hoping to sell some paintings on the trip. The girls have got a couple of gigs, one at the art gallery and one at the Old Greek Hall in town, and they're going to film a video clip on the beach—you know, desert girls and the sea. Very deep and meaningful. From what Sellie tells me, you can afford to stay at the Plaza, ay.'

'Yeah, I s'pose, but what about Rolf?' Jock asked.

'We'll take him up in the service lift,' said Chloe. 'Come on, let's get you settled in, and then you can tackle Franklin. Who knows, Selina might bob up soon.'

Jock decided it was time to sound like he knew what he was doing. 'If he knows what's good for him, Franklin will talk,' he said.

'Have you got lockjaw?' asked Chloe.

'No, I was trying to be tough—you know, in the movies all the gangsters talk out the side of their cake hole.'

'You'd better get a gang first,' Chloe smiled grimly.

'I got a gang, Chloe. There's you, and Hiram, and Women's Business, and a trained blue heeler. We're laughing.'

'Ha, ha, ha,' Chloe replied.

And so they went to the Plaza, and smuggled Rolf up in the service lift. They took two adjoining rooms, but Chloe left them off the computer, and prepared to keep their presence secret from management. After all, somebody from the hotel must have given Briian Selina's home address, and it wasn't Chloe.

By 4 pm, Jock was ready for the show-down with Harold Franklin, Minister of the Crown and suspected kidnapping collaborator. He opened the roll-bag, put on a pair of light green trousers and a mauve shirt with a hammer and sickle print in yellow, and accompanied Hiram and Rolf to the foyer of the government offices.

Jock instructed Hiram and Rolf to stay put and read the magazines. He gave his name as Briian Bodoni to the security man, and after a quick telephone call, was told to front up in the Minister's office. As he entered the lift, it occurred to Jock that he should not have told Hiram to read magazines. It could well trigger some new entrepreneurial disaster.

The lift doors closed, and Jock entered the belly of the beast, a luridly dressed knight without a flame-thrower to his name.

7

Confess, Minister

Inside the government offices, the air-con took care of any residual effects of the humidity outside, and Jock felt the sweat on his back dry during his elevation to the ministerial offices. He didn't have a clue what he was going to say.

Harold Franklin was pacing around his office, causing several employees of Tourism to glance at the ceiling in an agitated manner. So far, the plaster was holding.

Franklin had banished Gavin Baskerville from his inner sanctum, and waited for Briian. What the hell was Bodoni doing here? He was supposed to be stashing that sheila on the *Effie*, his ocean-going gin-palace moored several hundred metres off the coast from East Point. It was more private there than near the yacht club.

Franklin was wearing his usual size twenty-four off-white nylon safari suit. He had taken the jacket off and hung it on a minature pandanus in the corner of the office next to the bookcase full of official-looking stuff he had never read. The jacket could easily have been mistaken for a marquee at a Packer wedding. This left him in the Territory politician's 'uniform', a white shirt with a white singlet visible underneath, and Territory flag collar studs. The Territory flag, in ochre, black and white, carried an artist's impression of the desert rose, a black circle with white petals. Colloquially it was known as 'the arsehole with teeth', which also applied to Franklin.

Slightly brain-damaged from alcohol abuse, he had retained much of what he had learned before he began drinking—including rat cunning, greed, narrow-minded racism, and a hail-fellow-well-met politician's skill for shaking hands and remember-ing everyone's name in an electorate that spanned several thousand miles, but contained only a couple of thousand people.

His face was flushed, and his huge belly strained at his shirt buttons. The ligaments in his knees were feeling the weight. Franklin turned and looked out of his window at the docks and Darwin harbour. The tide was way out, exposing mud and mangroves for hundreds of metres. Beyond, the sea was like azure glass. Franklin surveyed his domain.

He had to think of a way to get the girl killed— what was he saying?—or at any rate put somewhere where she couldn't be connected to him. And there was the small matter of that ABC bitch and her memory, which could return at any moment. Still, so far, they had no proof that he was involved. If only the blokes hadn't been so heavy-handed. It wasn't meant to go like this. Why couldn't they have just grabbed the plans?

Franklin farted loudly, and smoothed a hand over both hairs on his head. Although he wasn't thinking about it at this moment, Harold Franklin did not have a single friend in the world. People were paid to be polite to him, say yes to him, laugh at his blue jokes. His voters thought he was a decent, down-to-earth sort of a bloke who wouldn't try siphoning taxpayers' money into a shonky merchant bank—an image he worked hard on. But nobody who knew him well actually liked him. Not even his wife.

The intercom on his desk blatted smartly: 'Mr Bodoni to see you, sir.'

Franklin smiled briefly at the thought of Connie, his secretary. He knew she didn't like being patted on the arse whenever it took his fancy, but she still had to call him sir. And he couldn't see any sexual harassment legislation coming her way.

Feeling good, feeling tough, feeling in control, Franklin took a green can from the bar fridge underneath the bookshelves, snapped the top open and waddled back to the desk to press a button on the intercom. 'Send him in, Connie love.'

He took a pull on the beer, flopped down on his chair and dislodged half a kilo of plaster from the ceiling underneath. At the first sound of Franklin's chair protesting, the clerk underneath snapped open a golf umbrella, and the pieces of plaster skittered off the umbrella and rained around him.

Upstairs, Franklin's door opened, and Connie, being careful not to break a fingernail on the door-handle, missed the Minister's look of bafflement when he saw Jock.

'Coffees, Minister?'

'No Connie, just piss off.'

'Yes, sir.' She closed the door behind her.

Jock moved to the window, put his hands in his pockets, and nodded. 'Top view,' he said.

'Who the hell are you?'

'Trouble, Minister,' said Jock. 'I am trouble.'

Further downstairs than Tourism, in the foyer, Hiram and Rolf were getting restless. Rolf had taken to herding all arrivals up to the security desk, which was regarded as a most charming trick by one and all. Hiram was tired of waiting around for all of five minutes. His scant survey of *Business Review Weekly* (which he insisted on called BR Dub) had whetted his appetite and heated his blood. It was time to wheel. Time to deal. Time to . . .

Hiram noticed a short, dark-haired bloke wandering about the forecourt of the government offices. He had several cameras slung around his neck, and was attempting to regain control of a fold-out map. A cog slipped in Hiram's brain, and as a result, the plot not so much thickened, as curdled.

Hiram revolved out through the door and grasped the man by his left elbow. He pumped

109

the man's hand in a killer handshake, and beamed. The small man smiled politely, and bowed. Hiram bowed back.

'I am Harasato,' said the man, with a slight German accent. 'Museum?' he added, pointing at the map.

'Hiram F. Doppelganger,' boomed Hiram. 'Glad you could make it, Harasato. Come in, come in. We'll get this thing sewn up and go and have nine holes to celebrate. Come right this way!' He propelled Mr Harasato, Toyota factory janitor from Kyoto, through the revolving door again. Mr Harasato was beaming. 'Yes, golf! Yes. Museum, golf. Ah, arigato.'

'That's right, matey, Arigato Finance, glad you could make it,' shouted Hiram, as he and Rolf shepherded the Japanese tourist to the security desk.

'We're here,' said Hiram to the security guard.

'I can see that,' the guard said, stony-faced.

'We're here,' repeated Hiram, his eyes alighting on a small notice-board near the stairs, 'for the development meeting, level four.'

'Righto, why didn't you say so,' said the security guard. 'Level four, glass doors on the left as you get outta the lift.'

'Come along, Mr Harasato, we'll give 'em a show,' said Hiram, striding across the marble to the lift, and folding up the map. Hiram had one arm around a beaming Mr Harasato, who was saying, 'Paul Hogan, koala bear, frill-necked . . . ' when the doors closed behind them.

Rolf looked at the security guard. The security

guard looked at Rolf. 'You're not wrong, pal' said the guard.

On the fourth floor, Hiram strode confidently through the glass doors, dragging Mr Harasato behind him. Luckily the glass was shard proof, and shattered into harmless glass pebbles. It caused quite a scene; shocked secretaries, and business-suited public servants, who had been poised to begin the meeting, hovered around uselessly. Finally, Hiram and Mr Harasato had shaken most of the glass from their clothes, and although Mr Harasato was somewhat unsteady on his feet, Hiram held him up.

Everyone at the meeting wore large tags with their name, status or profession clearly marked, which made Hiram's task a lot easier. He used nous, hearty handshakes and momentum to work the room. At one end of a huge table was an easel with an architect's impression of a large building on it. It looked to Hiram like a bunch of aliens had landed on a thirty-five-storey matchbox.

He and Mr Harasato sat together. The convenor of the meeting, a senior treasury official, assumed that they were with two of the press secretaries, who assumed that they were with the public service blokes. The treasury official outlined the building project, adding that it was probably going on hold indefinitely, because although the government was willing to stake half the develop-ment, nobody knew who could put up the other half, and a site had not been chosen. He winked. After about fifteen minutes of this, Hiram made his move.

111

'Gentlemen,' he said, as he lumbered to his feet, and cracked Mr Harasato between the shoulder blades, 'This is where me and Harry come in. For those of you who haven't met me, I'm Hiram F. Doppelganger, the brains behind Brisbane's civic development project, Koala Square in Broome, and half the Perth CBD. I've got the building boys in m'back pocket and Mr Harasato here is . . . ' Hiram paused, and glanced at Mr Harasato, who promptly took his photograph.

'Mr Harasato here *is* Arigato Finance. He can dance his way around Eurobonds like berloody Pavlova, and he's got a swag of feisty yen he'd like to chuck at the lot of you . . . Haven't you Harry?'

Mr Harasato nodded vigorously, and beamed. 'Golf?' he asked hopefully.

'Yes indeed, I wasn't going to forget. Mr Harasato here also states that his Gulf oil properties, owned in tandem with the Bahrain government, ought to be handy in the collateral department. Together we're prepared to kick in $360 mill, with myself as project manager of course. We've seen your plans and we like them. We want to be up and running by the end of the next Wet, and we've got the cash and the know-how to do it.'

Hiram looked around at the silent, attentive collection of public servants. Mr Harasato began handing out his business card, which said he was a sanitation engineer in Japanese. As a janitor, he wasn't allowed to use the Toyota logo.

On a roll, Hiram continued: 'We'll take initial equity, and float later, with government guarantee. It's as good as money in the bank. I've got a couple of big institutions that will come in or take equity.' Any questions?' said Hiram.

'Hang on a minute,' said a weedy treasury official. 'That's unsustainable, surely, in this economic climate. Which institutions? Can we talk to your bank?'

'Shut up, Jeffrey,' said one of the press secretaries.

'No, no, by all means,' said Hiram, adopting an omniscient expression. 'You can check me from bum to breakfast, sonny, I'll bring in the details tomorrow. But you know as well as I do that with a seventy-five per cent equity for the government it's not only sustainable, it's perfect. I'm not here to be insulted. I notice you've got a ring on there, son. Harvard MBA are you? Bit tragic for you, son. I've been making profits for thirty-five years, I've got the runs on the board. As Bobby Gottliebson said to me the other day . . . '

'Look, I'm sure there's no problem,' interjected another Treasury official, who was booting Jeffrey's shins under the table.

'Well, you've got twenty-four hours to decide after you get our bits of paper,' grinned Hiram. 'We're off to Singapore in a minute. I'm at the Plaza if you need me. Come on Toshi, let's go and have a look at the greens.' Hiram winked. 'And I'm not talking about golf. Chicago futures have just opened.'

'I'll just go and get a steno so we can get this together for a press release,' said Gavin Baskerville, and bolted from the room.

Jeffrey eyed Hiram, and asked, 'I suppose you've got documentation so we can tie this up?'

'Try me, my boy,' retorted Hiram good-naturedly. 'Now, if you'll excuse me?'

Along the corridor, Jock was having a little trouble with the Minister.

'Look, Minister, I know you know where Selina is and we want her back. Own up. Get real. Come clean. Do the right thing. We can cause a lot of headache for you. I can't think of any other clichés.'

'Who's we?'

'We may be a team of highly trained cracked terrorists. We may be a bunch of decent citizens with connections in high places. We may be a loose collective of ballroom-dancing fiends. That's not important. We are taxpayers, we vote, and we . . . bloody hell, what do you care?'

'I don't know what you're talking about,' said Harold Franklin, thoughtfully scratching his crotch. 'Now bugger off.'

'Oh, fabulous,' thought Jock, as he walked out of the lift and into an empty foyer. 'Get absolutely nowhere with porky-features, and now I've lost a patient.'

Jock revolved out on to the footpath, into a wet wall of heat. It felt like his brain was expanding, and there wasn't enough room in his skull. Unfortunately, it seemed to be the stupid parts of his brain that were getting bigger. The Build-up was making everything sluggish, and thinking straight was the first casualty.

He untucked his shirt, flapping the tails to circulate some air, and stared out across a big expanse of lawn sloping down to a cliff-top studded with palm trees and bouganvillea. The sea was beyond, bright blue and seemingly scattered with diamantés. Jock closed his eyes against the glare, and listened to the vibrating, scudding sprinklers, kshhh thwocka thwocka thwocka, kshh thwocka thwocka thwocka, which seemed to go non-stop all over Darwin. Darwin was not supposed to have lawn, mused Jock. Lawn was an import, like beer and guns, and—what had Franklin called him? An interfering southerner.

Jock stuck two fingers between his teeth and let out a big two-note whistle. He heard a faint, answering bark. He waited sixty seconds and repeated the whistle. Closer, he heard two barks. Rolf was having trouble getting back, but not enough to make it necessary to go and find him. Hiram was probably putting up a bit of an argument about being herded back.

As he perched on the edge of a heavy concrete flowerpot to wait, a white Commodore with tinted windows and an arsehole with teeth fluttering from its bonnet pulled up in front of the building, engine still running. Franklin waddled out through a side door, and got into the back seat. Across the road, Jock noticed a man in the shadow of a palm tree. Despite the heat, he was wearing a brown suit and tie, and the kind of sunglasses that Jock's old friend and colleague Eric Urbanburger used to call 'FBI issue shades'. Jock smiled. He hadn't thought of Eric for a while. 'I wonder how he's going on the celebrity shrink circuit in the States,' Jock thought, before he spotted Hiram leaping around the corner of the building, closely followed by Rolf, who was nipping his heels.

Before greetings and complaints could be exchanged, Gavin Baskerville strolled out of the revolving doors, and slapped Hiram on the back. 'Mr Doppelganger,' he beamed. 'It's all fixed. If you'll bring in your documentation tomorrow, we'll get things organised and hold a press conference in the afternoon. You must meet the Minister, Harold Franklin. I'll schedule something for tomorrow. Who's this?' he indicated Jock.

'That's my nephew,' said Hiram. 'I think I'll take a walk back to the Plaza. Come along, Frank, we'll have to have a look at those Tokyo figures.'

Jock opened his mouth. 'Yes, Uncle,' he said.

Gavin Baskerville watched them go.

By this time, Selina was sitting in the kitchen of Franklin's floating gin-palace—she refused to call it a galley—and had found various ways of amusing herself while parts of the thug brigade were upstairs (or 'on deck' as they liked to say) drinking beer and playing checkers.

She had twice used her hairpin to tell the boat's computer to lift anchor, and had only desisted when advised that she would be struck repeatedly if it happened again. She had pickpocketed all the thugs' keys and hidden them about her person, written a note and put it in an empty Limmonaya vodka bottle (found in her secret compartment) then thrown it through a porthole which was unfortunately closed at the time. The subsequent racket had attracted the notice of her captors, who retrieved the bottle with the help of a long broom handle with a thingy on the end of it (the boat hook). She had also spent some time making up silly songs, mostly about how small Briian's willy was, and sang them to sea-shanty tunes as loudly as she could.

Usually she had no truck with conversations about willy size, and couldn't care less about it, but although she had never seen Briian's, she knew he would not enjoy her lyrics. She was particularly pleased with herself for rhyming 'Yo ho ho and an extremely small member' with 'it's even more miniscule in November'. She was also smug about managing to link 'liniment' with 'after-dinner mint' in a prurient and anatomically inadvisable fashion.

She had tried sending telepathic messages to Miranda: 'Hello there young girlie, get out of it. Hope you're all right, you always were hard-headed, please be all right.' And to Jock: 'You know I'm not interested in Briian, you lunatic psychiatrist, ring the police.' And to her mum and dad: 'I'm all right, I'm all right, I'm all right, how's Hetty?'

She had talked the thugs into letting her go upstairs (on deck). The usual watery Darwin vista greeted her. A couple of navy patrol boats were bringing in long convoys of Indonesian fishing boats. This lot had been after shark fin. They cut the fins off and used the rest of the shark to attract more. The shark fins, once destined for soup and now for a Fisheries Department bonfire, hung on lines all over the dilapidated fishing boats, like car-yard bunting. Oh well, there were dangers in hitch-hiking. Selina knew from Miranda's reports that the boats were often riddled with cholera, Yellow Fever and typhoid. Her frantic waving elicited only mirror responses, and made her even more over-heated. She had already polished off three litres of water, hoping that the thugs would get pissed on their beer and fall overboard.

The Build-up humidity was increasingly oppressive and the sun pretty heavy going. It sort of defeated the purpose of 'coming up for air'. It was more like coming up for some invisible soup. She stared thoughtfully into the water. She knew what was down there: sharks; salt-water crocodiles; deadly stinging jellyfish, and lots of them. If she made it to the shallows, there might be sting-rays that could slam a barb through a leg as soon as look at you. On land, she might get scrub typhus from the parasites in the long grass, and there was stuff in the soil that could come up through your feet and kill you. The locals called it 'Nightcliff Gardeners' Disease'. She could get Ross River fever from a mozzie bite, and the thugs still had guns, and a boat with an engine. Selina did not feel like a swim.

Briian sidled up, dressed in reflective sunglasses

118

and a navy-blue sports jacket with 'nautical look' gold buttons. He leaned against the rail, which only came up to the top of his thighs. On Selina it was about bottom-rib height. 'Look, just take it easy, babe,' he said. 'We'll just keep you out here for a while, and then when all the fuss dies down, hey, we'll let you go.'

'Briian,' replied Selina. 'You are not in charge here, and one of the very good reasons for that is that you sound like a particularly dicky episode of "Division Four". One of those blokes may have killed Miranda, and I saw it. Thirdly, and ergo, they will probably kill me. Or, as I read in a book once, ergo fuck yourself.'

Briian leered. I'm sorry, but he did, and quite frankly at this stage of the novel we shouldn't expect much more of him.

'A book, Briian. B double O K. You know, kind of like a video, but with less pictures,' Selina said.

Briian lowered his voice. 'No, I was just thinking, we've got all this time to kill. Franklin won't be here to talk to us for another hour or so. And you're the one who mentioned sex. I was just wondering . . . ' Briian wiggled his eyebrows and rolled his eyes in the direction of downstairs (below deck).

Selina looked at him speculatively. She lowered her voice too, but left her standards in a holding pattern.

'Wondering what?'

'What do you say, cupcake?' he asked.

'I say: shark bait!'

She pushed him overboard.

Djambin Till the Break of Day

Jock smuggled Rolf up to his hotel room by the back stairs and left him in front of the telly watching Floyd cooking half a bison. Going down again, he shared the lift with another man in a sharp brown suit and FBI issue shades.

'Lovely day,' said Jock.

'Sir. Yes, sir,' replied the man in the crew cut.

'On holiday from the States?' inquired Jock.

'Affirmative.'

Jock headed for the foyer bar shaking his head. His brains were fried, and there seemed to be a robot from Salt Lake City on the loose in the lifts, so he might as well throw in some alcohol to help him think. He might have been a Pants Man, but he eschewed ordering any of the cocktails named for a sexual experience, and asked for a beer instead.

'No, I don't want any lemon in it, for Chrissake . . . Look, sorry. Bad day.' He strolled to a table, put his feet and his beer glass on it and leaned back into a bit of interior forestry. He closed his eyes and tilted his face towards the ceiling.

When he opened his eyes and looked at the table his beer was gone. In its place was a baseball cap with CIA embroidered on the crown. He closed his eyes again and said, 'I'm hallucinating.'

A Los Angeles accent corrected him: 'Shorts, you son of a bitch! You couldn't hallucinate if you tried.'

Only one person ever called him Shorts, a silly extrapolation from Jock to Jockey to Jockey shorts. Jock opened his eyes, fast and wide, and before him stood a vision in a lurid purple Hawaiian shirt.

'Eric!' shouted Jock. A few other drinkers stared, including the matching pair of suits at a corner table. Eric and Jock embraced boisterously, causing a serious shirt clash.

'Yowwwwwwwwww!' shouted an ebullient Eric, who resembled nothing so much as a short viking. 'What the hell are you doing here, Jock? I was going to come and surprise you in Melbourne, after a real vacation in Kakadu National Park. You look like hell.'

'Urbanburger, I have rarely been happier to see anybody in my life. I'm in deep shit. I feel like I've walked on to the plot of a Z-grade movie, and you're the kind of crazy bugger who can help. Tell me why you're here and I'll spill the whole story,' said Jock. 'And give me my bloody beer. Good God, man, what are you drinking? It looks like an explosion in a fruit shop.'

Eric Urbanburger was also a crazy psychiatrist, but he had a better excuse—he was from North America. He was known coast to coast on cable television and talk shows as the TV Shrink. He had an opinion, and a shirt, for every occasion. Hostage crises, Madonna's love life, divorce in the suburbs, pets. He had made a lot of money and was very famous for being on the television. People came up to him in restaurants and told him how crazy they were, and asked for his autograph. This was America. He was a busy man.

Eric filled Jock in on the recent events which had led to his voluntary exile from the United States. It seemed that Eric had suggested that the American public send its dog shit to the White House. 'Solve two problems at once,' he said straight into the camera. 'Clean up the streets and let the President know he's full of it.' He informed the fifty-four million viewers of 'Morning In America' (and its affiliates in forty-three states) that the President was a howling mad, dishonest, power-crazed psychopath with a penchant for secret killings. He went on to explain that the President used to be the head of the CIA, and therefore obviously used to be, and probably still was, involved in shady and shocking stories in Central America, South America and elsewhere. His intelligence background would have necessitated lying, he saw war as something to be entered into voluntarily with a minimum of discussion, and therefore he was completely unhinged. Much of Eric's eloquent and credible explanation was not broadcast because the director of the programme

122

had cut to an advertisement about canary headache tablets and was shrieking through the studio intercom to get Eric off the set.

'MAD PREZ?' headlines and current affairs programmes devoted to the sanity of the nation's leader followed, and the White House hosed it down as best they could. The Washington postal service was complaining, and more crap was being unloaded from the White House than usual, if you didn't count the Iran-Contra affair.

Eric found his syndicated columns cancelled, his regular talk-show spots rescheduled, cut or unused, and two agents from the American Federal Bureau of Investigation on his tail. He called them Heckle and Jerk Off; they had followed him for three weeks, all the way to Australia, and were now sipping orange squashes in the corner of the Plaza foyer bar.

Jock and Eric waved at them. Heckle and Jerk Off pretended not to notice. Jock mimed talking into the cocktail umbrella he took from Eric's drink, and Eric answered on one of his shoes.

It was easy for them to fall back into their friendship. Jock and Eric had met at an international symposium on psychiatry in Hawaii. They were the only attendees at a seminar called 'Psychiatry: What's The Point?', and the lecturer hadn't turned up. The men would have gravitated to each other anyway. At registration time, they were the only psychiatrists wearing rit-real Hawaiian shirts. During the typical photo sessions when delegates showed each other photographs of their wives, husbands, and children, Jock showed pictures of

Rolf, and Eric indicated a surgical scar on his knee, a legacy of a grid-iron match in his teens.

The two men had gone about having a very good time at the conference. They applied themselves to the task and the local night-clubs and women whose names ended in 'i', and later occasionally sent each other postcards from bizarre places. Jock would get one from Truth or Consequences, New Mexico, and Eric would get one from Woy Woy, New South Wales.

'Eric,' said Jock. 'I'm in trouble. I fell in love . . .'

'Damn right you're in trouble. Shoot, Shorts, I warned you about stuff like that,' Eric replied, trying to take a sip of his drink and getting half a banana and a pink plastic flamingo in his ear.

'That's not the problem. Look, we can't talk here. Come up to my room.'

So they went. Rolf liked Eric straight way, and Jock told him the whole story about Selina, and Briian, and Miranda, and Franklin, and the kidnapping.

'Wild,' said Eric. 'Totally, like, wild.'

'Don't come the raw Valley Girl with me, mate,' said Jock. 'In the movies, this is where we're supposed to say, "Wait, I've got a plan!"'

'Can't we be in one of those movies where they say, "Hey, kids! Let's put on a show"?' complained Eric.

'Wait!' said Jock. 'I've got a plan!'

'Oh, cool.'

124

Miranda sat up and twisted around to look at the top of her bed, which had a label with her name on it. A nurse appeared at the end of her bed.

'Hello, nursie,' said Miranda.

'Welcome back to the world,' said the nurse. 'You've slept a long time.'

'Am I sick?'

'No, just an amnesia patient. Well, not really amnesia, just concussion. You should be well on the mend after that long sleep.'

'Yeah, I'm remembering now,' said Miranda, noticing the nurse's name tag. 'What are my chances of getting a beer, Pete?'

'Nil by mouth,' he said.

'Amuse me further.'

'The police guard is here to take you home. You lucky thing, there's been two gorgeous, burly blokes hanging around in the corridor waiting for you for hours.'

'I can't say I'm particularly thrilled, Pete, I bat for the other team,' winked Miranda.

'Oh wacko, all the more for me,' said Pete. 'I'll just go and find Dr Feelgood and get you discharged.'

'Tell me my doctor isn't called Feelgood,' asked Miranda.

'Have it your way, doll. You can get dressed now.'

Two hours later, Miranda had been interviewed and looked through a large book of mug shots at the Berrimah headquarters of the Northern Territory Police. She hadn't seen anybody she recognised as part of the thug brigade.

'I'm sorry,' she said. 'It was pretty fast, and all

these blokes start to look the same after a while,' she indicated the books. 'I'm supposed to be a trained observer, and I'm not doing very well.'

'It's OK,' said Constable Djambin, who was sitting across the table. 'Maybe they're southerners.'

The police had told Miranda about Jock's suspicions that Briian the Crazed Architect had been present, but she couldn't help. 'I don't know what he looks like, except Sellie said he was a sleaze. I'd recognise the guy who punched me again, though. They called him Ken. But his picture isn't here.'

'Well, maybe we can rustle him up through contacts interstate. As for this Bodoni bloke, we wanted to see if you could pick him in a line-up, but apparently he's checked out of the hotel for two days. We told him to remain available, so he's sus already. Thanks for your time. We'll give you a ride home, and I'll be outside your place until morning, just in case.'

'Really? All night?'

'Commissioner's orders.'

'Oh, right, Chloe, of course. What do you reckon the chances are of finding Selina?'

'I don't know, Miss Spurn. This is a weird one. I usually just pick up drunks and talk to Neighbourhood Watch meetings.'

'An honest cop?' Miranda smiled.

'Stop trying to suck up to a potential contact in the force, Miss Spurn,' he smiled back.

'Ms or Miranda, take your pick. Am I that transparent?' she asked.

'Like a negligee in a horror movie, Miranda' he replied.

'You're wasted on Neighbourhood Watch, Constable Djambin. With that kind of flair you should at least get a crack at media relations.'

'Yair.'

Miranda arrived home at dusk to a full house. The lounge-room was covered in swags and so was the verandah. Chloe was boiling a large billy-can on the stove.

Everyone was very pleased to have Miranda home again, particularly since she bore no ill effects of her jaunt into silliness except a plaster on her head.

Miranda sat on the kitchen bench and handed out apples to the kids while she talked to Chloe who was cooking beef. The women sat out on the verandah and sang songs belonging to their skin groups. It was almost relaxing, if Miranda and Chloe hadn't been so worried about Selina.

'Well, I don't know about this Jock fella. He's better than Hiram, who's obviously two sandwiches short of the full picnic,' Chloe said. 'I think I've got more faith in the coppers on this one.'

'Yeah. I'll go into work tomorrow and see what I can dig up. The problem is that I'm known to be having a dispute with Franklin. I can't accuse him of a zoning fiddle land scandal unless I've got the proof, and they took the copies of the plans with Sellie,' Miranda thought out loud. 'But I can make him think I know more than I do.'

'What?' asked Chloe.

'It's one of the two more reliable tricks up a reporter's sleeve,' replied Miranda. 'You pretend you know more than you do, and the other person lets slip some stuff they think you already have. The other way is to pretend to know nothing. This is particularly effective with the blokes who think they're brilliant. They fall over themselves patronising you and explaining everything to show how clever they are. Their guard is down and they tell you dangerous things they don't think you'll understand.'

Chloe smiled. 'Yeah, I get it. Well, be careful. You've already had your noggin cracked once.'

'I'll be careful. Anyway, Franklin can hardly hit me in his office, can he? I'll set up a nice, sedate interview.'

'Speaking of sedate,' said Chloe, 'the band has scored another gig. Apparently some federal minister is visiting tomorrow, and there's a do on at the yacht club. They want us to do a set and some dances. Will you come? And can you get us some publicity on the radio?'

'Yep,' said Miranda. 'Maybe a night out will do us good. Chloe, I think I'd better ring Sellie's mum and dad. They should know as much as we do.'

'I met Jock at the Plaza this arvo. He's already called them. But he said to tell you they're worried about you too, so you should give them a ring. They're coming up on the weekend if she hasn't turned up by then. By the way, there are no copies of the plans left in the architect's room. He must have taken them with him.'

'Chloe—how do you know that? You used to be a real terror on hotel rules,' said Miranda.

'Rules. Since when have rules helped us?' Chloe

128

replied, carrying the tucker on to the verandah.
'Bring those tongs with you.'

Selina was lying on the deck of the gin-palace
looking at the stars, trying to occupy her mind
with plotting her Mills and Boon novel, *Hornrims
of Desire*, but she was worried about the muted
conversation downstairs. Franklin had been in
there about half an hour, and his motor boat bobbed
next to the stern. They had taken something out
of the engine so she couldn't commandeer it.

She knew the talk was about her future. The
longer she was in captivity, the more heat would be
generated on Franklin and Briian the Crazed Architect. That's all the place needed. More heat. She
wondered if they would run to a pair of concrete
pumps, or if they'd just hurl her overboard and wait
for her to drown or become some reptile's lunch.

She couldn't quite make out the words, but there
seemed to be an argument going on. Briian's voice
was loudest, almost hysterical. She wondered if he
was arguing for or against her survival.

Selina concentrated on the plot of *Hornrims of
Desire*. She briefly considered changing the title to
Wing of Desire and adding a pilot heroine, but the
title sounded too much like an Aussie Rules football
position. Her brain raced through an imaginary
commentary. 'Yes, young Timmy Godlike is coming
in all on his own from the wing of desire, AND

IT'S A SCREEEAMER! What do you think, Douglas, can he put it through the hey diddle-diddle?'

God, what was happening to her brain? She forced herself to concentrate. Right. OK. Deep breath. *Hornrims of Desire*. Short, intriguingly bespectacled Range Bancroft, well-muscled owner of his own earth-moving equipment hire business, meets Hoyden Pert, red-headed, greeny-grey eyed, willowy librarian, when she demands that he return his borrowed copy of *Fat is a Feminist Issue* because it's three months overdue.

'Can you bring it in?' she asks him huskily, a pulse beating at her ivory throat.

His voice grows hoarse. 'Nay,' he snorts, stamping his foot.

'Hey, Blue,' a voice interrupted.

Selina opened her eyes.

Ken was unzipping his trousers, and taking a leak over the side of the boat. Selina closed her eyes again and briefly prayed for a sudden change in wind direction. It made her feel powerless, and she began to cry, silently, so that he wouldn't be able to tell. This in itself was an unsatisfactory arrangement, because the Law of Grief and Gravity says that crying on your back means your ears fill up with tears.

The thug was saying something. Selina shook her ears clear, and said, 'What?'

'The boss is going to have a word with you shortly. Alone, if you catch my drift . . .' He smiled, and it was not attractive. Selina immediately pulled herself together. Now here was something. If she was going to be alone with Franklin, she'd at least have something to work with. Enough of this romance nonsense, she told herself. Action stations, girlie. Get out of it.

She sat up, and brushed her fingers through her hair, which was bringing new meaning to the word tousled. The thugs shuffled up on deck, looking sheepish. Briian wouldn't look her in the eye. 'Sorry,' Lefty muttered, as one of the thugs jerked his head in the direction of the hatch. He seemed to be in a vile temper.

She went down the stairs backwards, turned, and saw Franklin sitting squished in at the edge of the small kitchen table, with half a bottle of whisky and a glass in front of him. 'Minister,' she said.

'Selina, isn't it?' said Franklin, with what he thought was a smile. 'Come and sit down. Get yourself a glass. I thought we'd better have a conflab about your position.'

'Oh, God,' thought Selina. 'That's a political term, is it?' She sat down opposite Franklin, uncomfortably close, and topped up his glass. She poured a small one for herself. Franklin took the bottle and sloshed some more into hers.

Selina glanced to her left, and saw that the double bed had been turned down. 'He's got to be joking,' she thought. 'I'll fight like hell if that's what he's got in mind.' She thought about the men outside and shuddered. She knew she could do a lot of physical damage before she was overpowered, but she also knew that her greatest strength was not physical. She looked at Franklin.

'Are you going to kill me?' she asked.

'Oh, look, really,' he began, with the tone he employed at press conferences when somebody asked a sensible question and he was trying to indicate that it was really absurd.

'Shit,' said Selina. 'You're going to kill me.' She felt the world contract, slide, and then she focussed again.

'Well,' began Franklin, conversationally, 'I don't see that we can avoid it, since you put it that way. You've recognised me, and the lads. Frankly I don't give a rat's what happens to them, but I can't afford to weather a kidnapping rap. I don't think even the venerable local paper could editorialise support for me after that. What we do want from you, of course, is co-operation.'

'Oh, yeah, great,' said Selina, 'Shall I polish the bullets for you?' She heard her voice as if it came from somewhere else. This was real, but it didn't feel real. Her will was concentrated on showing no fear.

'There's a chance I can convince them to leave you alone if you show a little co-operation,' sleazed Franklin.

'Hey, do I look like Patty Hearst?' she retorted.

'Who?' said Franklin.

'Come off it, Minister,' she said, trying to keep reminding him of his position and not sure if that was going to work for or against her. 'What could you do for me? Would you trust me not to go to the police?'

Franklin smiled. 'I'm very good friends with the police. And it would be your word against mine. And I am a Minister of the Crown.'

'He is supremely arrogant', Selina thought. 'He really believes he might be untouchable.'

'And, my dear young lady, we could come to an arrangement whereby you agree not to say anything.'

'Why would I arrange that?' asked Selina.

'So we wouldn't have you killed,' explained Franklin.

'I like that arrangement,' said Selina.

'But then again,' mused Franklin, 'it would be messier. And you might try and get witness protection.'

'But you're a Minister of the Crown,' said Selina bitterly. 'You could find me.'

'Yairs,' said Franklin. 'But, as they say, you scratch my back, and I'll scratch yours. And,' he added, in a way he thought was seductive, 'I've got an itch.'

Selina tried not to throw up. 'Focus,' she said to herself fiercely. She knew what she had to do.

'Minister, you look all worn out,' she said. 'Why don't you have a little lie down, and I can make it worth your while.' She smiled at Franklin, hating his every cell. He smiled back, and wobbled to the bed, causing a slight pitch in the yacht. He began to unveil a rather pudgy storming of the palace. Selina drew on everything she had. She let her voice drop deeper, ready to work his ego. She had him where she wanted him.

'Now,' she said. 'Let us begin.'

Yo Ho Ho and a Green Can

'Just relax, Minister,' said Selina soothingly.

'Don't try anything funny,' murmured the great white whale in Y-fronts. 'Remember those blokes upstairs. Now listen. Last time we went to Hong Kong for industry talks, I met this little girl in a bar who could do this thing with ice cubes . . .'

'Nothing to worry about,' she murmured, wanting to be sick but moving on to the edge of the bed. She was wearing a T-shirt and a sarong, and wishing she had a suit of armour. It was time to go to work.

'Wanna try something really kinky?' she asked.

Franklin, lying flat on his back, tried to see past his stomach.

'What do you mean?' he asked, suspiciously.

'Well, you've heard of phone sex, haven't you?'

134

'Yeah . . .'

'I'll just talk to you for a while, and then we can get down to business. Anything you like, OK?'

'Righto,' replied Franklin. 'I like my girls to talk dirty to me.'

Selina breathed deeply, blessed her lucky stars for meeting Keith Tremble, and began to thoroughly hypnotise the Minister.

By the time she'd finished with him, he was convinced that he'd had fantastic sex, that Selina was not to be killed under any circumstances, and that she was on his side. Additionally, the next time he tried to have sex he would experience intense pain in his genital region. In case of emergency, she equipped him with a secret code word. If he ever heard that word again, he was to take off all his clothes and forget who he was until the second code word was given.

Selina cradled a slab of beer in her arms and jumped up and down about five times to simulate what she guessed accurately, was Franklin's idea of bonking. The boat shook and rolled. Then she woke up the Minister and thanked him for the beautiful experience.

He never even took off his Y-fronts.

After explaining that Selina was to be treated well, Franklin barrelled off across the water in his motor boat with a dopey grin and a green can, steering rather erratically with one hand. Selina too, was smiling. Briian couldn't believe it. Lefty looked keenly at Selina, but she smiled back sweetly. She had used her time below deck to take stock of the secret compartment in her hat-box.

135

She had three tampons, a picture of a fireman, half a dozen condoms, some KY jelly, a miniature bottle of vodka, and a pack of cards.

'Canasta?' suggested Selina.

'Yeah, why not,' replied Lefty.

Selina, Lefty, Briian, and Ken spent the next hour playing cards. Selina moved the deck around, through the table, and found twenty-cent pieces in Ken's ears. She bent spoons and bamboozled Ken and Briian with sleight of hand until they retired, frazzled. She and Lefty stayed up for a while. Lefty told her what the stars were, and she taught him a couple of easy card tricks. When he said he thought he should become a card sharp, Selina smiled, said he'd need a dinner suit, and beat him at poker five times. They sat for a while in companionable, overheated silence, eventually broken by Lefty.

'I dunno what you did, but I'm pretty sure you didn't . . . you know . . . with the boss,' he said awkwardly. 'You're all right for a girl.'

'So they tell me,' said Selina. 'Goodnight, Lefty,' and she took her swag and hat-box down to the front of the deck to set up camp. 'I hope one of you is going into town in the morning for supplies. I could seriously frighten some scrambled eggs for brekky.' Selina dreamed fitfully of Hawaiian shirts and preserves.

Thursday 17 December 1998

It was another beautiful sunrise in paradise. Miranda saw it because she was on early shift. Selina saw it because it woke her up. Miranda had to get to work, and Selina had to escape, but only Miranda got the job done that day. She had to take the breakfast shift, because another new ABC announcer had shot through without warning.

The problem was at least as old as the regional radio station itself. Jobs for the ABC had to be advertised nationally, and out-of-work and disgruntled announcers from down south invariably thought they'd be able to get away from their families, start a new life, soak up some sunshine, or get over a broken heart in the Darwin office. Occasionally, they got the job. Some of them lasted; most didn't, especially the ones on the off-peak shifts. They got lonely, they got pissed, they realised that they carried their problems around between their ears or they eventually got a job somewhere else without mosquitoes, ninety-five per cent humidity, a playlist with Cat Stevens on it and exactly the same weather report for six months of the year followed by cyclone warnings.

Sometimes they'd have boozy farewells and promise to write. Years ago, one had even thrown a party, the highlight of which was the huge pile of beer cans that reached almost to the ceiling of the lounge-room by 4.30 am. One of the punters had dived into it, sliced his eyebrow on a ring-pull and was rushed off in an ambulance, followed by a string of undetected over .05 offences in small

Japanese cars. In those days, it wasn't a proper party without a trip to casualty. Signposts to the Darwin Hospital are extremely prominent. The acceptable blood alcohol level in the Northern Territory was .08, not .05 as it was elsewhere; it was considered political suicide to tamper with a citizen's unalienable right to get utterly legless and drive home.

Anyway, this latest disc jockey just hadn't turned up for work the previous day. He'd left a note on his desk which read, 'Gone. Sorry'. Nobody minded much; he had made a dork of himself during his three-week stay, including the time he'd burst into tears on air after playing Rod Stewart's sensitive masterpiece 'Hot Legs'. 'That's for Sheree,' he had sobbed. 'Wherever you are, ma-a-a-te.' He had then fallen insensible with grief under the panel where he was retrieved by the emergency technician, who had drunk bourbon and played 'Jingle Bells' for an hour and a half and missed the Sydney link with the current affairs programme 'AM' before anybody noticed. It was a measure of the announcer's popularity that nobody bothered to ask him who the hell Sheree was.

The station manager had shaken his head, faxed off the same advertisement, and offered Miranda some extra work in the interim. It was a good break for her because she got off work at 9 am and had the rest of the day to tackle Franklin. She waved goodbye to Constable Djambin, and drove to work.

Miranda plugged that night's yacht club gig at every opportunity. It was billed as a 'meet the Federal Minister for Mining evening'. The aforementioned pollie was on a typical whistle-stop tour to tell the Territory Government they only survived because of Commonwealth funding out of all pro-portion to the tiny population, while providing Territory politicians with an opportunity to sneer about ignorant, interfering southerners behind his back. None of this Miranda mentioned.

There was going to be a barbecue, dancing by the Nyampuju women, and a set by the popular band, Women's Business. She played their single, 'Country', twice, and blamed it on a computer error. At 8.59 she was relieved by The Clarrie Garter Hour, kissed it on the top of its bald head as she adjusted its headphones, and was on her way out the door with a tape recorder by 9.01.

'Good morning, gardeners,' said Clarrie into the microphone, blowing her a friendly kiss.

Miranda stopped off at the Plaza for a free break-fast and a short chat with Chloe to see if there was any news from police HQ. There wasn't. Chloe waved at a man in spectacles and flamingo pink. 'Miranda, Jock; Jock, Miranda.'

'Well, hello,' said Miranda. 'We'd better get together and discuss some tactics for finding Selina. I'm . . .

'Hello,' he said. 'Sorry, I've got to run. I'll see you later.' Miranda raised an eyebrow and watched him go.

'Well, I'm off too,' said Miranda. 'Into the cock-roach's den.'

'Cockroaches don't have dens,' retorted Chloe.

'They have big, shiny buildings and potted plants,' said Miranda. 'Wish me luck.'

'Go with strength.'

'I like that.'

'Gwarn. Make the bugger squirm.'

Miranda got past the security desk by tipping the security guard a wink. She had given his daughter some work experience a couple of months ago, and the girl had stopped talking about marrying a bikie and gone off to Sydney to learn journalism. He buried his nose in a copy of *More Trucks Galore* and whistled ostentatiously while she waited for the lift.

At Franklin's secretary's desk she paused.

'Wow, Connie, you look better than I've ever seen you!'

Connie grinned, moving her chair back and putting her feet up on the desk.

Miranda gasped. 'Connie, good God, what's happened! Army shorts?? Where are your stilettoes? What did he say when he saw you?'

'He hasn't yet. I feel fantastic. My cousin rang from Newcastle yesterday. My aunty died and left her a small business, a milk bar near the beach. She wants me to come and help run it. So, my notice is on his desk.'

The lift opened again, and Franklin waddled out, for once not noticing Connie's legs. At that moment, the fire-escape door opened, and Jock and Eric appeared, in pink and chartreuse shirts respectively.

'Morning,' said Jock.

'Ah shit, not you again,' said Franklin.

Miranda took her chance. 'Minister, I wonder if I might have a word with you about . . .'

'Shut up,' growled Franklin.

He turned to Connie. 'Keep these dickheads outta my office,' he said, feeling powerful, feeling good. 'And get some clothes on, cunt.' And into his office he lurched, slamming the door, leaving behind three dropped jaws and an implacable Connie.

'Jeeez-us,' breathed Miranda. 'The sooner you're on that plane the better.'

'Miranda,' said Connie. 'I have spent the last year or so keeping you out of his office, lying to you about whether he's in, and what he's really thinking. I can't count the number of times he's called you that. Now that I'm a free woman, let's go and have a drink.'

'It's nine o'clock in the morning!' Miranda remonstrated.

'It's quarter past nine, ladies,' said Eric.

'Who are you calling ladies, weasel-dick?!' snapped Miranda and Connie in unison, then flustered their apologies.

'Sorry, you're copping some of the flak that in-there deserved,' Connie said. 'I'll be back in a sec, Miranda.'

'No offence taken,' said Eric. 'Why don't you two run along. We've got some business with the Minister.'

Miranda raised an eyebrow (it was her specialty) at Jock.

'Run along?' she asked him.

'What my esteemed colleague meant, Miranda, is . . .' He watched Connie nick into the women's toilet, oblivious of her duties as office watch-dog.

141

'We've got a plan, so piss off for a while.'

'Jock, I don't know you very well, but I think perhaps . . .' she eyed their shirts with obvious distrust.

'Miranda. Get out of here before you get involved in something a journalist can't be involved in. I'm serious.' He gave her a sincere, committed sort of a look.

Miranda snorted. 'Sellie told me you were good with the charm. Don't do anything illegal. I'll try and see if Connie will leak me the files, but it's not going to be easy. She could lose her entitlements.'

'What?' said Jock.

'Never mind.'

It had not occurred to Miranda that Jock and Eric would really do anything illegal, which was a rare slip-up in the instinct department. On the way out of the building, Miranda noticed Heckle and Jerk Off, who were wearing plaid and ostentatiously photographing the building. She and Connie shook their head, for different reasons. 'Not spunk material', said Connie's shake. 'Mormon toyboys', said Miranda's.

Jock and Eric stood outside Franklin's door and looked at each other.

'Right, little buddy,' said Eric. 'What do we do now?'

Jock thought for a moment. 'I don't know.'

'Hey, I don't want to cramp your style, pal, but when you said, "I've got a plan", I kinda assumed it was the sort of plan which provided a "what do we do next mechanism". Call me crazy.'

'Perhaps "plan" was the wrong word. Maybe I should have said, "concept". You have to admit, it's a good concept. I mean, kidnap a Minister. That's daring. That's audacious. That's . . .'

'Hoo boy,' said Eric, as well he might.

'Do you think he'll come quietly?'

'In my professional opinion?'

'Yeah.'

'Not a chance.'

'We'd better hurry, before someone else turns up.'

'Please,' said Eric, 'don't say "While the coast is clear".'

'Oh, all right.'

'We haven't got a chance. We'll be in jail by ten o'clock.'

'Right, that's settled then.'

The two men burst into Franklin's office.

Hiram was sitting in the Minister's chair, and the Minister was stark naked, staring out the window.

'Oh my God,' said Jock.

'Oh my Gard,' said Eric.

'Greetings, lads,' shouted Hiram, cheery as ever, chewing a cigar and trying to light a match on the sole of his shoe. 'Just been having a little meeting with the Minister about our development. Seemed to be going pretty well, until he decided to conduct the rest of it in the nuddy, and pretend he doesn't know who he is. But hell, the corporate world's gotta move with the times. I'm a New Age kinda guy, I can dig it. I only buy cans of dolphin that are tuna safe, and if it takes a crystal up me clacker to close an eighty-seven million dollar deal,

143

I'm game.' He leaned back in his chair and put his feet up on the desk.

Jock was staring at Hiram, and Eric was staring at the enormous Ministerial blubber.

'He's catatonic,' said Eric, by way of explaining an inexplicable situation.

He walked over and gingerly waved a hand in front of Franklin's face. Franklin waved back.

'Hiram,' said Jock slowly, 'Do you know why Mr Franklin took his clothes off?'

'Hell, no,' said Hiram. 'But I will. I'll get his tactics beat if it's the last thing I do. I remember when Rupert and I were battling it out in Aspen for . . .'

'Hiram,' interrupted Jock. 'We haven't got much time. What happened just before he took his clothes off?'

'We were just having a preliminary chat, boy, before getting down to the nitty-gritty, tin-tacks, the bare bones of the deal. I was telling him about my new yacht and suddenly he started taking off his strides. I did inquire, but he denied being the Minister, and so then it became a war of nerves. I'm just waiting for him to crack.'

'I think he's already cracked, Hiram,' said Jock.

'Hey, I've got an idea,' said Eric. 'It seems to me that the Minister needs some psychiatric help.'

Jock, in his professional capacity, agreed. They decided to take the Minister to the hospital.

While Hiram tried to dial a fictitious number in Berlin, Jock and Eric tried to dress the Minister, but he wouldn't have a bar of it. They began to get very frustrated.

'We haven't got much time,' Jock said.

'You've said that,' snapped Eric. 'Any minute somebody's going to come in and think we're having some kind of orgy.'

'I've got to think,' said Jock.

'Enough with the clichés!' said Eric. 'What happened to this guy, anyway? One minute he's the golden boy of the joint, and then, abracadabra, he's a walking moron!'

Jock was about to say he was usually a walking moron anyway, but at the word 'abracadabra', the light returned to Harold Franklin's little reptile eyes.

'Fuck!' he shouted. Everyone else jumped.

'What am I doing without my strides? Give me those,' he added, swiping his trousers from Eric and putting them on. With one leg in, he fell over into a chair, dislodging three kilos of plaster and the last straw for the clerk downstairs, who brushed dust from his blotter and began to write his resignation letter.

Hiram rose to the occasion. 'Minister, you may feel a little confused. You appear to have had some sort of breakdown. I have summoned this small, discreet team of my personal physician and his assistant.'

Franklin looked at the two men in absurd shirts. 'But then again', he thought, 'it doesn't seem any more cock-eyed than standing around my office in the nuddy with no recollection of the last ten minutes.' Jock and Eric tried to look professional.

'Minister,' said Jock. 'I think you should accompany us to the hospital for a couple of tests.'

But Franklin was suspicious. A successful North-

145

ern Territory politician is good at remembering faces, and Franklin could hardly overlook the fact that this man had been in his office hardly twenty-four hours ago, demanding to know what had happened to Selina.

'Hey, what is this?' he asked. 'You were in here yesterday, asking me about . . .' he trailed off.

'About what, Minister?' asked Eric.

'I don't think so, sir,' added Jock. 'I've just flown in this morning from Maui on the express wishes of my employer, Mr Doppelganger. And you may examine my credentials.' Jock flipped open his wallet and proved to the Minister that he was a psychiatrist.

'What does he need a psychiatrist for?' said Franklin, indicating Hiram.

'Corporate tactics, Harry,' boomed Hiram, coming around the desk to thump him on the back. 'This little crew psyched out the directors of victims in more hostile take-overs than I can count. Now, let's get you down to the hospital, eh? You can't be taking off your clobber at all hours of the day and night. And then we can get this little deal wrapped up at the meeting scheduled for later this morning. We've wasted a lot of time.' Hiram winked at him.

Franklin was disoriented and deeply worried, but he still possessed a certain amount of cunning. 'Yeah, OK, but I'll go myself. Can I give you blokes a lift somewhere?'

Jock saw his plans (not to mention his concept) crumbling, but agreed. 'Yeah, sure, you can drop us at the Plaza.' The four men left the office, and

146

took the lift to the basement, where Franklin squeezed in behind the steering wheel and gunned the engine of his executive car. The air-conditioning blasted off immediately. Eric was in the front, Jock and Hiram in the back. Franklin swung the wheel wide on the exit from the government offices while Jock whispered furiously to Hiram.

Hiram was getting cross, and began to raise his voice. 'I tell you, it had nothing to do with me. I was telling him about my new yacht, and about how the upholstery got worn out on the other one. I just told him I'd decided to keep the same name, and he started the bump and grind act, only without the bumping and grinding!'

'What's that?' asked Franklin.

'What was the name of the boat, Hiram?' asked Jock, urgently.

'It is not a boat, my dear boy, it is a 67-foot luxury yacht!'

'What's the bloody name of it?!' shouted Jock, who had ceased to worry about the effect of indulging his patient's every fantasy.

'Oy, settle down in the back,' said Franklin.

'What's it to you?' retorted Hiram.

Jock leaned over and grabbed the lapels of Hiram's only suit, which according to Hiram was one of thirty-two exactly the same. 'What is the *name*?!' He figured there was nothing left to lose. Everything was too scary, and he might be able to claw back some control if he could get Franklin to make like a Nembutal overdose case again.

'SERENDIPITY!' shrieked Hiram.

The car veered on to the shoulder gravel, the

back fish-tailing slightly, and stopped with an almighty jerk. While Jock, Hiram and Eric were still slamming into the seats from the sudden stop, Franklin was out the door, standing on the side of the road taking his shirt off.

'You bloody beauty!' shouted Jock, hurling himself out of the door and pushing Franklin into the back seat, where he continued to disrobe, a very distressing experience for Hiram, who didn't have much room left in which to breathe.

Jock jumped into the driver's seat and slammed the door. 'Ho for the hospital!' he shouted.

Eric had buried his head in his hands. 'We're going to be struck off. We're going to jail. You can't be *serious*! Jock, have you got *any* idea what we're going to do when we get to the hospital?'

Jock, concentrating on not being crushed by a road train which was passing him on a curve, didn't answer. Possibly because they were all in the same vein, he didn't answer any other questions from Eric as he followed the signs to the hospital, and pulled up in the car park. He looked at Eric.

'What do you say we commit a Minister of the Crown to the psych ward for a day or so?'

'Sure. Do you think there'll be room for us as well?' asked Eric.

Unnoticed, another car pulled into the lot, and stopped in the far corner. Heckle and Jerk Off settled in to wait.

Chloe phoned Miranda's place and arranged to spend part of the afternoon helping her sisters and aunties and mothers arrange their dot-dot paintings under one of the yacht club verandahs. As well as the dancing, they hoped to make some money from an impromptu art sale. Next, the band equipment was set up for Women's Business, and a sound check run.

Selina was below deck, sweating. The thug brigade, bored witless, was going into town, all except Briian, who knew the police were looking for him to 'help with inquiries'. Lefty wanted to look in the classifieds for a second-hand dinner suit. Selina was hoping that somehow she could use Franklin's hypnotism to her advantage, and congratulated herself on choosing two unlikely code words. Nobody in their right mind was going to say 'serendipity' to Franklin, much less 'abracadabra'. But she would feel a lot more comfortable if she knew she had some smart operators on her side. She crossed her fingers and hoped.

At that moment, Jock and Eric were standing in a quiet corridor of the Darwin Hospital wearing white jackets they had found in a cupboard. Harold Franklin was sitting on the floor of the cleaner's room behind them, singing 'I Did It My Way' in a whisper. Hiram, instructed to wait in the car, had driven it back to town, followed by Heckle and Jerk Off at a regulation FBI distance.

'Look,' said Jock. 'I haven't got a clue how we can sneak him into the hospital. But we can't hide him in the Plaza, can we?'

149

'Well, we'd better do something quickly,' said Eric. 'Or we'll both fry.'

'Fry? We don't "fry" people in this country, Urbanburger. We're civilised. We throw them into a black hole of hopelessness and violence for a few years and expect them to reform. Look, OK, the psychiatric ward's down this way. We can put a sheet over his head and say that's a manifestation of his psychosis.'

Eric sighed. 'He's the deputy-whatever-you-call-it, Shorts. The matron in charge at least is going to get a look at him. And secondly, we're in a strange hospital and how the hell do you know where the psych ward is?'

'I'll sweet-talk the nursing staff, mate, leave it to me. And secondly, I know exactly where we are because this hospital is exactly the same design as the one in Canberra, where I did my internship. It's even got the snow-slides above the windows.'

'Bullshit. This is the tropics. What do they need snow-slides for?' Eric looked out the window across the corridor. 'It's got snow-slides.'

'We haven't got time to discuss the small minds of the health bureaucracy and great architectural cost-cutting measures of our time, Urbanburger. Now get a sheet over his head, and wait for me here. I've got to make a phone call.'

Jock strode around the corner to a public phone and was back in five minutes. Eric was almost hysterical.

'What are you *doing*? I'm stuck in a cupboard committing a felony with a gross jerk who thinks he might be Frank Sinatra! Who were you calling?'

150

'The newspaper.'

'Are you crazy?!'

'I was just placing a personal ad. You know, like in *Desperately Seeking Susan*. Selina's a magician's assistant. That's what gave me the idea. Just like in the movie. Except I was offering a straight swap: Selina for Franklin.'

'Oh, that's just fantastic! What does the ad say, we've got the Minister for Zoning in a straight jacket and can we have your girlfriend back? I do not *believe* this!'

'Don't be ridiculous, Urbanburger, it's in code. I just made it. It'll be in the afternoon edition. They're going to press in ten minutes.'

'Code,' repeated Eric, dully. 'Wake me up when it's over, will ya, buddy?'

Matron Rosie Minjawirra looked up from her desk to see two somewhat dishevelled men and a figure covered with a sheet.

'Good morning,' said Jock brightly.

'G'day,' she replied, poised with her pen above an official-looking form.

'I am Dr Jock Jovanovich, and this is my esteemed colleague, Dr Urbanburger, from St Harvard Hospital in America. We've got a teensy problem I hoped you could help us with. This is a patient of mine from Melbourne, who escaped from a mental institution. We'll need him sedated for a couple of days until I can arrange alternative accommodation for him.'

'He looks pretty sedate to me,' said Rosie.

The enormous figure in the sheet writhed a little, and pulled the sheet down around his ankles.

151

'M-O-yooooo-S-E, MICKEY MOUSE!' it sang.

Rosie looked at a naked Harold Franklin and put down her pen. Then she looked at Jock and crossed her arms.

'I hope you don't think you can sweet-talk your way out of this one,' she said.

Hiram strode into the development meeting and shook hands with Gavin Baskerville.

'I don't know where the Minister is,' said Baskerville, 'I'm sure he won't be long, Mr Doppelganger. It's very unlike him. Please—have a seat.'

'I've just left him,' replied Hiram. 'He seemed pretty pleased with my proposal, finance-wise. He said something had come up, and to carry on without him. Anyway, I understand that your department is PR, laddie, so we should be able to handle that between us. Now, I think we should go with the line that this is a revitalisation of the Territory's economy—maybe start with a strategic leak.'

'I like it,' said Baskerville.

'The thing is, Matron . . .' began Jock, in the only private patient room in the psych ward. 'The thing is . . .'

'The thing is,' said Rosie, standing at the end of the bed sagging under Franklin's weight, 'you are an unaffiliated doctor who has just materialised with the Deputy Premier who appears to have lost his marbles, and you seem to be suggesting that nobody in authority be informed. You have been here for an hour and a half and you've come up with four different accounts of how he got that way and why he's your patient.'

A buzzer sounded.

'Excuse me again,' said Rosie, on her way out the door. 'I'm trying to run a psychiatric ward on the side.'

'Ten years,' murmured Eric, slumped in the chair beside the bed. 'We're going to get ten years for this. Don't make up another story, Jock, for God's sake.'

'I've got her wrapped around my little finger,' began Jock. 'Everything's going to be . . .'

Rosie re-entered the room wearing rubber gloves and holding a kidney basin with a syringe in it. 'Hurry it up,' she said. 'I've got to help somebody go bye-byes.'

'You see, Matron, it all began . . .' said Jock, grinning most boyishly.

'Cut that out,' said Rosie.

'Fifteen years,' mumbled Eric.

'It's patient–doctor privilege,' Jock continued. 'Just before he went catatonic, the Minister told me that he doesn't want anybody to know. He said that this happens once every seven years, it will last twenty-four hours and he'll be fine again. You wouldn't want him to jeopardise his career, would you?'

'Jeopardise his career?' asked Rosie. 'If I saw him covered in honey I'd tie him to an ants' nest and set fire to his nasal hairs, but that's not the point. Obviously the man is suffering from some deep trauma, or else he's insane. But he is *not* violent, and therefore I cannot authorise sedation.'

'Matron, I am authorising sedation. I am a doctor.'

'Not in my ward you're not. I've never seen you before in my life. You just appeared in my ward with a major scandal, and I didn't even say 'abracadabra'.

Franklin roared to life, his eyes fixed on Jock. 'You bastard!' he shouted. 'I'm not telling you anything! You can't get me! I'll kill you first!' He ran towards Jock, and the room shook. Bedpans clattered to the floor, and the bed chattered on the lino. Franklin clamped his hands around Jock's neck and squeezed. Eric screamed and tried to pull him away, but it was like trying to get a lamb chop away from a hippopotamus with lockjaw.

Rosie plunged a hypodermic needle into Franklin's arm, and his hands slowly lost their grip. There was still light in his eyes, but it died when Jock recovered his power of speech. 'That was a bit of serendipity, eh, Matron,' he croaked. 'Lucky you had the business with you.'

Franklin went quiet again.

Eric bit his fingernails.

'Despite the fact that the Minister is sedated,'

she said sternly, 'I shall have to ring his wife, at least.'

She could not be persuaded otherwise, and after looking up the telephone book, made the call from the telephone next to Franklin's bed, pressing the conference button so they could all hear the conversation. Eric was pacing up and down, and Jock looked nervous.

'Hello, Mrs Effie Franklin?' said Rosie. 'This is Rosie Minjawirra from Darwin hospital.'

'Has there been an accident?'

'No, no, it's all right, your husband has not been in an accident.'

'Rats.'

'Pardon?'

'Nothing,' said Mrs Franklin, looking out at her harbour view.

'Er, it seems he may have had some sort of nervous breakdown,' said Rosie. He is under sedation here, and a Doctor Jovanovich from Melbourne says he is handling your husband's case. He further says that he thinks it best if this information be kept from the authorities and the Press until at least tomorrow, when he expects to be able to talk to Mr Franklin again. Do you know this doctor, Mrs Franklin?'

'Let me talk to him,' said Mrs Franklin, a look of concern crossing her face. 'Hello?'

'Hello, Mrs Franklin,' said Jock. 'He's in the best possible care, I assure you. We met last year, at . . . um . . .' He shut his eyes tightly and held his breath.

'Never mind that,' said Mrs Franklin. 'Can you keep the mongrel away from me until tomorrow?'

Jock opened his eyes. 'Ah, yeah. Yeah.'

'Good. I don't want any reporters snuffling around here. Keep it quiet for as long as you can.'

'Would you be wanting to visit, perhaps?'

'Not on your nelly. Give us a call tomorrow, ay? I've got at least one night of freedom and I don't want it buggered up,' said Mrs Franklin, and put the phone down.

'I don't know what's going on here, but I'll respect Mrs Franklin's wishes until tomorrow night, if there's been no change in his condition,' said Rosie. 'After that, the law says he's got to have a hearing in front of a magistrate, and I think that will pretty much be the end of all this secrecy.'

The phone rang.

Franklin answered it.

'Am I Dr Jovanovich?' he asked vacantly.

'No,' said everybody crossly, and Jock took the call.

'Uh-huh. Uh-huh. Uh-huh,' he said. 'Yacht Club, 7 p.m. I'll be wearing a blue Hawaiian shirt. Yep. No funny business,' he added, and hung up.

Rosie left, saying something about other patients to deal with.

'I know I shouldn't ask, but who knows you're here?' said Eric.

'Just the crooks,' said Jock proudly. 'We've got a meet, tonight. Should be a nice, quiet spot, but it's a public place.'

'Didn't you listen to the radio this morning? Miranda was plugging the "Meet the Federal Mining Minister Party" at the yacht club tonight.'

'The more the merrier!' announced Jock.

156

'And Shorts,' said Eric patiently, 'Don't you think, now they know we're in the hospital, that they'll come and, just for argument's sake, let's say, mow us down in a proverbial hail of bullets?'

'I don't know any proverbs about bullets,' replied Jock. 'And anyway, they'll never guess this is where we've got Franklin.'

Franklin snored.

'Oh, gross,' said Eric.

10

Selina Not Seen Dead in Flares

During the afternoon, Hiram entertained a journalist from the *Territory Voice* in Jock's room at the Plaza. Not just any journalist, but Felicia Caxton, chief political reporter and editorial writer. Felicia was extraordinary in many ways, firstly because she claimed to be related to Evita Peron, secondly because she was a fifty-year-old unmarried woman who tried to seduce every new male cadet on the paper, thirdly for her unhinged adoration of the Premier, which had culminated in a public love poem over his policies last Christmas, and also because she was the only chief political reporter in the entire country whose analysis consistently showed more faith in government policies than that shown by the government itself.

While this made the government happy, it could

be an embarrassment when its own enthusiasm was overshadowed by a hearty bi-weekly editorial proclaiming an imminent economic fiesta revival party-time. She had thrown a huge party when the Northern Territory had gained statehood, on the same day the Government announced plans to mine national parks and halt any further Aboriginal land claims.

Although the government flunkeys were awaiting final proof of Hiram's holdings, and had only signed an in-principle agreement with him, Felicia knew she was on to something. She'd had a little whisper from inside the government offices that something big was on, and a fair idea of what it was. She presented herself at Hiram's door at the Plaza, produced a perfumed notebook, became instantly infatuated with him, and proceeded to ooze questions at him, including, 'How does it feeeel to be the saviour of the Territory economy, Mr Doppelganger, or could I call you Hiram?'

Hiram prattled on with a string of lies that fell well within the parameter of silly as a wheel.

'This will make a doozy of a front page,' thought Felicia. In that, at least, she was quite correct.

'Just call me Scoop!' she thought deliciously to herself. Actually, they called her Floppy-drawers, but that's beside the point.

Felicia smiled, and leaned towards Hiram. 'You *are* a fascinating man, ' she said.

'Yep,' said Hiram, cheerfully. 'More raspberry lemonade?'

Out on the boat, the thugs were discussing the plan to swap Selina for Franklin. Lefty held a copy of that afternoon's paper well out of Selina's reach and read from the 'Collecting' classified column: 'Friends of Harold: Wanted to swap. Swap card of old political figure for rare bird. We want the magic back in our lives. Change your plans, you can't do without it! Phone . . . blah . . . blah . . . blah . . . You don't need to know the rest.'

Selina looked up through her fringe. 'I don't understand,' she said. She was sitting on the deck with her legs dangling over the side.

Briian explained: 'They've got Franklin, and we've got you. He's gotta sign some papers before midnight tomorrow. They want to swap. It's totally ridiculous. This whole thing has got completely out of hand. It was just meant to be a simple zoning fiddle, and now look at it.' He glared at the thugs. 'Kidnapping, assault,' he added.

'So what happens now?' said Selina, wondering who on earth her allies could be. Miranda? A team of cracked ballroom dancing fiends? She shook her head. 'Are you going to swap? You can't close the deal without Franklin's signature, Briian. Who are you working for, anyway? They don't want to be mixed up in this, do they?'

Briian looked over the side. 'We're going to go and get Franklin from them, Selina, and you're going to stay here. So am I, since the cops would like to talk to me. It'll be just you and me while the fellers go off and deal with your little friends.'

Selina supposed she could have retorted with something a lot more witty and sophisticated, but

'Yuk,' pretty much covered how she was feeling. They would disable the radio, but she had lifted the key to the emergency cupboard. Maybe she could work out how to fire a couple of flares. It happened in films all the time. She wished she had paid more attention to the flare-gun scene instead of the hot sex scene in *The Big Easy*, and although it might be a little melodramatic to shoot somebody with a flare gun, in Briian's case it might be worth it. She shook her head. It wouldn't do her much good, the others would only come back and she'd be in the bad books for causing human collateral damage. But a flare in its traditional role— an SOS, Mayday, come-and-berloody-save-us-we're-sinking sort of message, that would do nicely. She would wait until it was dark.

The sunset switched on around 6 pm, with the usual purple clouds and orange orb business. Parts of Kakadu National Park were burning, and the sunset had an extra red tinge. Rangers had set the fires (following generations-old land-management practices of the Gagadju people) and invisible airborne ash added to the show.

Down on the waterfront, the breeze fanned those seeking some relief from the humidity. Public servants and ministerial advisors in their white shirts, shorts and absurd long socks and sandals were more used to the air-conditioning of their offices, homes and cars. The yacht club grounds, around the barbecue, were filling up rapidly with people who had taken a shower after work and started sweating again immediately: Greek and Aboriginal families, East Timorese refugees,

Chinese, the whiter-than-white and sunburned, hippies, journalists, film crews, the pious and the pissed, in sundresses and thongs, safari suits and sarongs.

The Minister was a little late, having been detained by telephone calls from his working-class electorate in Melbourne, a small portion of which had been blown up in a chemical waste explosion during the afternoon. The Minister's flak-catchers and hose-downers were checking out the crowd, getting the diplomatic lie of the land, and making sure that if important ethnic representatives or lobby groups were lurking around, they would be beamed at and have their right hands clutched by a federal minister (unless they were Timorese).

Women's Business were making short work of a few jugs of lemon squash with their mums and grans and aunties at one of the tables off to the side; like the vast majority of Aboriginal women in the Territory they were teetotallers. Soon the dancers would go off to an area hidden from the yacht club precincts by pawpaw trees and poincianas, and 'paint up', lining their faces and breasts with white clay.

All the dancers wore red 'mission-style' or 'modest' skirts. Dancing boards, flat, elongated ovals covered with dot-dot paintings denoting skingroup totems lay in an unceremonial heap on the table, but they were not interchangeable. Each dancing board was a title to land, to stories, geographical knowledge and spirituality. Elsewhere, similar dancing boards were in museums and art galleries, protected from dust and probing fingers, and in a controlled environment. A few canvasses were spread out on the grass for sale, and some fighting clubs and grey blankets most Australians would have called 'horse blankets' lay heaped at their feet.

The women had no direct competition for tonight—often, away from home at festivals and special events, they danced on the same bill as their desert neighbours of Yali. There was much rivalry between them, a rivalry that was judged by a very different criterion by others every time the television cameras were there. It didn't matter if the Nyampuju women danced perfectly, or had the right owners of the right stories leading the singing. Not when the Yali dancers, albeit equally skilled, wore feathers in headbands for their ceremonial public dancing. They would get the thirty-second grab on the TV news, because they looked just that tad more 'exotic'. No matter that their dances would go unnamed, their homes mispronounced, their own contribution unacknowledged by name. They looked like Aborigines are supposed to look, only more so, according to the news editors.

Print journalists and photographers whose work went south also knew the score. Out bush on a story? Get a photograph of an Aborigine in a telephone booth. If you could persuade some poor old bugger to take his trousers off and grab his spear, even if he wasn't going hunting until tomorrow and had planned to fill out his tax return instead, so much the better. Standing in his undies listening to the dial tone would do it.

Near the dancers, a gaggle of greenies was having an argument about whether to hang a banner between two poinciana trees. 'Trees have rights too,' announced one, who had recently changed her name to Seedpod, after a succession of others, amongst them Indigenia, Endangered Scrofulous Wallaby and Ozone.

'Oh, God,' murmured the president of the Environment Protection Force, who despaired at having to deal with every blow-in air-head who had once attended a rally in Launceston by mistake and considered it less important to take on the corporate giants with some semblance of cohesion than to write very bad poetry about rain forests set to stolen Joni Mitchell tunes and sing it in shopping centres.

Darwin was wall-to-wall with them in the Dry season, grown-ups putting on improvised dolphin dancing displays with broomsticks and a ukulele and calling it community theatre, or embarrassing the well-organised conservation groups. Most of them shot through during the Build-up, pissed off to Byron Bay or somewhere cool, but this one had proved unusually tenacious, owing to a liaison with a local musician.

'Shall we ask the bloody trees, then, Kylie?'

'My name is not Kylie,' she retorted. 'I've asked you twice to call me Seedpod, so don't try and oppress me with your fascist sexist narrative, Louis'.

'Well, I gave it my best shot.'

A few sensible environmentalists came to his aid while Seedpod was dispatched to stare in

164

raptures at a piece of driftwood on the beach. Louis remarked that it never ceased to amaze him that people could actually smoke marijuana in the tropics. It made them so laid-back they were practically comatose. He snapped back to action.

'One, two, three, heave!'

The banner was hoisted: reading 'Hands Off The Wilderness' in fluorescent orange on white, with the O in 'Off' replaced by a picture of the sun with a smiley face on it. Louis began to distribute pamphlets about the likely effects of a cyanide spill from a gold or platinum mine getting into the river system of a national park as the Minister left the car-park and approached the assembled thongs. He was wearing a Hawaiian shirt he had bought during a vital seminar on wheat sales in Waikiki, in his earlier incarnation as Minister for Rural Affairs and Improbable Junkets. He figured it would put him in the tropical mood, and his polyester safari suit had been decorated by the sauce from a hot dog he ate at the crocodile farm earlier in the day.

Louis managed to get a pamphlet to the Minister, who smiled absently, said 'We'll look into it—it's a matter of great concern to the Government and myself,' without glancing at it, then turned to his host, the local federal member. 'Not a bad turn-out, Bluey,' he remarked.

'Nothing but the best, mate,' said the local member, who had used the term 'mate' forty-six times that day already.

The Minister was steered around and intro-duced to various people as the sun was sucked down below the horizon. After a few minutes stars appeared in the dark purple–black sky. At the counter-tea cash register, a woman with more tattoos than teeth took control.

'Yair, whaddayawant?' she asked, as she wrote down the order, glanced at a piece of paper in front of her, and pressed a microphone button.

'Number fifty-six, number fifty-six, your dinner is ready,' crackled the speakers hung from trees with bits of bent coat-hanger. The barbecue cranked up, and the smoke blew upwards to disappear against the stars.

The Minister came over to meet the younger Nyampuju women.

'And this is the lead singer, Ivy,' said the local member.

'Hello Ivy,' said the Minister.

'Hello Minister,' said Ivy. 'Enjoying the campaign trail?'

The Minister laughed very loudly. 'Oh, the election's a long way off yet,' he said.

'So any talk of an early double dissolution is just a salacious rumour, is it?'

'Us fella mob bin working hard for you fella in Canberra,' the Minister said brightly over his shoulder.

'You know,' said Ivy as she sat down, 'I'm not sure that the recession was entirely our fault after all.'

The Minister continued his rounds, startled by the sight of a famous fashion designer from America, who had come to the Territory to 'learn' from Aborigines, in other words, rip off their totems

166

and designs, mass produce them on 'leisure wear' sewn by exhausted Filipinas in a locked factory and sell them in First World chain stores for outrageous prices. The Minister was mostly startled because the designer had been off in the bushes with the Nyampuju women who had let her play with their ochres; the result was a White Californian blacked-up with brown ochre. A few local women like Chloe were getting ready to deck her.

'Who does she think she is, Al Jolson?' muttered one.

The Minister beamed at Chloe. 'Hello, how are you?' he said.

'Fine thanks.'

'Looking forward to the dancing?'

'Yep.'

'It's always such a marvellous treat to come all the way here for some Koori culture. Marvellous.'

'They're not Koori, they're from Nyampuju,' she said.

'Oh, well, of course, let me just say that I mean Koori in the wider sense, as you people have asked to be addressed.'

'I've never asked to be called a Koori in my life,' said Chloe. 'That's a word used for Aboriginal people in the south-eastern states. There's Murris in Queensland and Nungas in South Australia and a whole lot of different names for groups all over.'

'Extraordinary,' said the Minister. 'And what do you call us?'

Chloe tried not to laugh. 'Excuse me, I see some friends,' she said.

A couple of late-comers caught her eye. Jock

had excelled himself in a sky-blue Hawaiian shirt covered in wood-block printed pineapples. Eric had chosen to dress down for the occasion, in a black cowboy shirt with purple contrasting pockets, cuffs, collar and shoulders. At least they were both wearing suits. Jock's orange, cut in a baggy forties style, and Eric in a sharp, electric blue.

'Making a video?' Chloe asked.

'Hi, Chloe,' said Jock. 'How goes it?'

'Any news?' said Chloe.

'No,' he winked, 'but we might have some by the end of the night.'

Chloe sighed. 'Sure. Well at least the cops are still on the case. I've got to go and see the ladies. I'll find you after the dancing, OK?'

'Yo,' said Eric.

'You speak my language, brother,' smiled Chloe. 'See youse later.'

The timeless sound of a person saying 'Chuck. Cheque, wuntoo' into a microphone drew their attention to the makeshift stage between two trees. Women's Business, with their backs to the sea, were ready to go.

Ivy, on guitar and up front, kicked in with a long wailing note, and then the others joined her. They belted out their song, 'Country', which their record company was trying to get radio stations to play. It was in a mixture of Kriol, language, and English, a reggae-influenced number which had a few people affecting a self-conscious bop. By the fourth song, paradoxically a favourite cover of Territory rock bands, called 'The Ballad Of Lucy Jordan', more people had started dancing. The little kids were up the front. The girls finished their set with the hard-rocking 'You Ain't Nothing But A Camp Dog (Mangy All The Time)', and an invitation to attend their next scheduled gig.

The band walked past the Minister and the member, giggling and reaching for their water jug on the table. 'Marvellous!' oozed the Minister. 'You really ought to consider doing that professionally, girls!' The local member rubbed his forehead and grimaced at Ivy. She nodded.

The level of chat rose, but the sound of clap sticks and women's voices intruded, built, and quelled the noise. Out of the darkness, the dancing mob came, one by one, with little hops. The women formed into a line, pounding the dirt with their feet, moving in time. They sang of a bushfire, of collecting seeds to make bread, of a snake spirit. Their breasts, painted in white lines and loops, jiggled as they danced and their faces were concentrated and serious.

The audience was respectful, some people a little puzzled. This was not wild, exotic dancing, and the words were in a foreign language. Ivy took the microphone again, explained the meaning of the dances, and introduced the last one, a short celebration of a good day's hunting for bush honey. At the end, the applause was warm and trailed off into conversation and more orders at the bar.

'Number 56, Number 56, please collect your meal,' said the speakers.

Strangely, it seemed to get hotter after the sun went down. The humidity was almost stifling. Several people were getting outrageous-drunk, some were maudlin-drunk and some were shit-faced. The Minister took his suit jacket off. The hair-dos of professional wives drooped, and shirts stuck to backs.

Suddenly, a very tough-looking person appeared at the Minister's elbow. The man had a broken nose, and a very determined expression.

'Where's the Minister?' said Lefty.

'I am the Minister,' said the Minister, smiling, and holding out his hand to be shaken.

'Don't get cute,' said Ken. 'Where's the fat boy?'

'I beg your pardon,' said the Minister, 'Are you referring to the Minister of Defence?' He noticed two other thugs.

'Franklin,' said Ken. 'Don't play with us, sunshine, this is the big league.'

'Look if this is about the environment, really, we *all* care, we *all* have children, and it's important to realise industrial imperatives . . .'

'What kind of bullshit is this?'

'It's official policy.'

'Um . . .' said Ken.

'No real names, Ken,' said Lefty.

'There's another bloke over there with a blue Hawaiian shirt on, mate.'

'Shit,' said Lefty. 'So who are you?' he said to the Minister.

'I'm the Minister for Mining in the Federal Government. I'm on a "meet the people tour".'

'Shit, sorry.'

'No worries.'

'Briian, is there any more vodka in that cupboard there?'

'Wishwun?'

'The one with the red cross on it.'

'Lemme see. Um. Nup. Jush thish thing,' said Briian, taking out a small case.

'Let me have a look,' said Selina, taking the flares box from him. 'Oh, yes, here's some,' she continued palming the tiny bottle of vodka from her secret compartment and handing it to Briian. 'I'm just going upstairs to look at the stars.'

'You're a really good mate, Shelina,' muttered Briian, trying to bite the top off the vodka bottle.

'Uh huh,' she replied, grabbing a torch and heading up the steep stairs.

Jock and Eric stood up. Jock's knees were shaking.

'Woh,' said Eric. People are rarely eloquent in the face of three huge blokes in suit jackets with bulges under the arms. Lefty looked like he was considering shirt-fronting Jock, but he sat down on the opposite side of the table as Eric indicated. It took some of the cockiness out of him: he had to slide his bum in sideways on the bench.

'Now what's this about a swap?' he asked Jock, looking suspiciously at Eric then trying to skewer Jock with a scary look. Jock fancied that his knowledge of psychiatry might allow him to regard this gambit a trifle patronisingly.

'We thought we'd swap you Harold Franklin for our friend. We know you are keeping her somewhere.'

Lefty reacted quickly, grabbing Jock's lapels, jerking them open and then whacking him in the chest. 'You wired?'

'Hey!' protested Eric, trying to get on his feet. He was pushed down again by a thug extra, and the small skirmish attracted a little attention from nearby party-goers.

'It's OK,' said Jock loudly. 'Just joshing.' He lowered his voice and hissed at Lefty: 'Stop that!'

'You gonna make him?' sneered Ken.

Jock and Eric looked at each other, and then back at him.

'That's pathetic,' said Jock. 'I feel like I'm in kindergarten again.'

'Let me handle this,' said Eric. 'Hey, I can understand where you're coming from with this masculinist vibe,' he told Lefty.

Jock snorted.

'Eh?' said Lefty.

'Hey, we all need to go into the woods sometimes, rejuvenate our masculinist selves. But this is not one of those times. We must reconstruct.'

'Shut up, mate,' said Lefty.

'No, really, if you want to reach for the throbbing heartland of he-ness . . .'

'Oy.'

'I'm just trying to say we're men—brothers. What have you got that I haven't, how are we different?'

'There's this.'

'Yes, there's the gun thing, sure. Over to you, Jock.'

'Thank you my friend. We have the Minister.'

'Can ya prove it?'

Jock reached into his inside pocket. Lefty flinched. Jock pulled out Franklin's wallet and flashed it open.

'OK, that's all I want to know. Listen, pal,' he said, keeping his gun below the table but pointing it, presumably for reasons of logic, at Jock.

'What are you gonna do, shoot through a concrete table?' asked Eric.

'Don't be ludicrous,' added Jock. 'We'll meet you down at the dirt car-park at the bottom of the wharf road, tomorrow, 9 p m. We'll bring the Minister, you bring Selina. Straight swap, OK?'

'Go and get the Minister now, or I'll shoot your friend,' suggested Lefty.

'That idea really sucks,' said Eric.

Ivy appeared behind Lefty. 'See ya, Jock . . . hey, is everything OK here?' she asked.

'Piss off, girlie,' said Lefty.

Ivy took a step closer, looking at Jock and Eric's tight faces. Behind her, some of the older women gathered, ready to go home, blankets, fighting sticks, dancing boards and headbands in hand.

'I said, "piss off"!' said Lefty, moving the pistol so she could see it, but keeping it low so it didn't attract the attention of everyone at the yacht club. It did not have the effect he intended. Eight large-breasted, heavy-hipped, alarmed Nyampuju women began shouting at him.

'Tell 'em to back off,' he yelled at Jock.

'Nothing to do with me,' Jock shouted back.

Taken aback, Lefty waved the gun again. Attracted by the noise, the other dancers came running. One look at the situation and it was on. Seventeen dancers dropped their belongings, scooped up their fighting sticks and made threatening gestures, shouting challenges in language. The two other thugs stepped forward, hands on their guns.

'Shi-i-i-it!' said Lefty, scrambling out of his seat backwards, almost falling over the bench in the process. He made a move towards Ivy, who had stayed still throughout the ruckus. But the women would have none of it. They had given him a chance to calm down. They charged, shrieking, and started beating the hell out of the three of them. Jock and Eric sat, open-mouthed, watching.

The women drove the men out on to the beach, shouting at them all the while. The three turned and ran clumsily down the sand, pursued by a very determined mob of fighting women armed with heavy sticks.

The thugs jumped into a rubber dinghy, jerked the motor into a roar, and skedaddled, heading in the direction of East Point. The desert women stood at the edge of the water, eyeing it warily and shouting at the diminishing boat.

Suddenly, two flares lit the sky above East Point, obviously coming from the other side.

'Fireworksh!' shouted one of the drunks.

The Minister looked at the women on the beach, who were gathered together and talking about getting out of town as quickly as possible. 'Rubbish place,' seemed a popular phrase had the Minister cared to listen. He turned to the local member.

'Spectacular!' he said. 'Something to remember, eh? What was that dance called? Marvellous culture. Marvellous.'

In a house up the hill, Effie Franklin was playing cards with some people she had been to school with: an elderly hippie called Max whose long white beard was trailing in a glass of whisky, the deputy head of the Northern Land Council, Mrs Ruby Jarrmbinji, who was squinting at a straight flush in her hand, and Mrs Beryl Najinsky, the cleaning lady, who was stubbing out her eighteenth cigarette.

'Let's put on the Madonna record again,' said Effie. 'I want to dance.'

'That's only because you know I'm going to win this hand, you minx,' said Ruby.

'Well, there isn't any other reason for putting that bloody great mirror behind you, Rube,' retorted Effie, packing up her telescope with a decisive whack and bounding over to the stereo. As she passed the open window to the verandah, two flares exploded, spilling red across the stars.

Down at the yacht club, Miranda watched the flares fade away. She stood still for a while.

'Number 56. Number 56 you dopey bastard . . .'

11

Squeeze Me Baby, I am That Wettex

Not very many people got a lot of sleep. If anything, the humidity intensified, to be relieved only by a short, cooler period at dawn. All over the Top End of Australia, people tossed and turned, frowned and sweated, muttered and thrashed, drank and fought, fell into their swimming pools, sprawled on verandahs, sprayed themselves with pump packs of chilled water, put their sheets in the fridge before they made the bed, took three cold showers between midnight and dawn, anything, *anything* to feel cool and dry again.

Some slept while their brains digested the subliminal message of the air-conditioner, an insistent, meaningless hum that caused ratty brainwaves and dulled the mind, like the sound of trying to remember something, and coming up blank.

People who didn't have air-conditioners dreamed even more fitfully and disturbingly, of fires, and drowning, and of paralysis.

Children's foreheads were plastered with hair and sweat, and they whimpered, or dreamed of icy-poles and skylarking under the sprinkler. Babies cried. Men hit women, or reached for them tenderly. Women shrieked bitter sarcasm, or yielded to the weather, to the life, or, smiling wanly, to a lover. Lonely people cried, strung out people had anxiety attacks, active people felt sluggish, or plain catatonic. None of the old people in Arnhem Land would die of cold that night. Dogs sighed, and stretched out on their bellies on the cool of wooden floors and concrete verandahs. Coconuts hung heavily from palms, and flying foxes pissed on the washing as they swooshed overhead, destined for electric crucifixion on power lines. In a little while the sky would begin to lighten, the sun would come up, the clouds would gather and trap the heat. But now, everything was waiting.

Selina had to rig her mosquito net so that no parts of her body touched it, otherwise the mosquitoes would land on the net and suck her blood through the muslin. She was ragged-tired, mentally exhausted from the night's failed attempt to attract attention. Somehow, looking at the full complement of stars was a little soothing, and a tiny sea breeze kept her from feeling too much like a crab cooked live in a saucepan.

Selina thought that today was going to decide her fate. But it was unlikely that she would get any help. Something had gone wrong last night.

Someone had done something with Franklin and Franklin was needed to sign some document by midnight—today. If that deadline passed, she would have no value as a swap. 'By tonight,' she thought, 'I'll be free . . . or I'll be dead.' She was not a betting woman.

Harold Franklin was sedated in the Darwin Hospital. His wife, Effie, and her guests, who were usually banned on his orders, were tossing and muttering on various couches and beds in his expensive house.

Miranda slept well, after being up very late trying to get the water police to check out a suspicious rubber dinghy that might be in the harbour. 'What do you think this is, the *Rainbow Warrior* case?' said the duty officer at police headquarters. 'It's the middle of the night, and you're telling me that you can't give me any more information than "It looks suspicious"? Get out. Get some sleep. And get off the booze,' he added.

Miranda couldn't tell him that there was something going on with Jock, Eric and the men in the rubber dinghy, because she didn't know what Jock and Eric were up to, couldn't get them on the phone at the Plaza, and didn't want to dob them in until she knew what was happening. She couldn't risk getting them into trouble if that would mean more danger for Selina. It felt six kinds of weird to her, and she didn't know how to start unravelling it.

The police had been busy, sweating on three car crashes, several domestics, a swag of drunk drivers, the unfortunate discovery that the two tourists creamed by the road train on the hospital road during the afternoon had been a couple of agents from the FBI, which wanted to know were there any suspicious circumstances, and a couple of imaginative vandals who spray-painted 'It's all bullsh . . .' on the Supreme Court building before they were, as the police say, 'apprehended', or as the vandals would say, 'given a belt over each earhole and charged with wilful damage'.

Hiram snored the deep, untroubled, Plaza air-conned sleep of the chronic, guileless liar, and Felicia Caxton went to work, drank twelve cups of coffee, smoked sixteen cigarettes, and wrote the story that would lead the morning edition of the *Territory Voice*.

The first paragraph she wrote was: 'Deeply charismatic, ruggedly handsome mystery millionaire Hiram F. Doppelganger is poised to lead the Northern Territory out of the economic wilderness with a $760 million tourist complex to be situated in Nightcliff', which the sub-editor changed later in the morning to 'EXCLUSIVE. A $760 million tourist complex will be built in Nightcliff next year, rejuvenating the Territory economy [stop, new paragraph] The brains behind the venture is deeply charismatic millionaire, Hiram F. Doppelganger, [and it went on] who yesterday described the venture as "a sure fire thing". Mr Doppleganger is expected to announce details of the project at a press conference this afternoon with the Deputy Premier, Mr Franklin. He spoke exclusively to the *Territory Voice* yesterday. "Harold and I are one on this," he said from his luxury Plaza suite. "We met on the baccarat floor in Monaco last year, and . . .".'

Felicia went home to her city flat and eventually fell asleep in her clothes.

Jock and Eric spent the night at the hospital, in Harold Franklin's room. Jock slept on the couch, and Eric in a trolley bed appropriated from the corridor. The night nurse had indeed fallen victim to Jock's celebrated charm, poor thing, and had agreed to waive the visiting hour rules (but Pete always was an old softie). Before they drove out to the hospital, the two psychiatrists had dropped off another classified ad at the *Territory Voice* for the morning edition. It read: 'FRIENDS OF HAROLD. Sorry about the bad reception. But still wish to join with you for swap meeting. Same arrangement, call now.'

Worried about the stir their decidedly uncool exit might have created, one of the thugs had come into town before dawn and collected an early paper off a pile in front of a newsagency. There was a short account of the yacht club function on page three, with a two-column wide picture of the local member looking on as the Minister accepted a steak on a plate from a woman with more tattoos than teeth. The Minister had adopted banal photo-opportunity pose number seventeen, the 'she'll be right' thumbs up. It is not worth relating the caption underneath the photograph, but you may assume that it contained the phrase 'beefing up', or possibly, 'Meat, the people tour'. Let us draw a veil over such events and move on.

There was no mention of the fracas with the Nyampuju women, unless you count 'An especially spirited performance'.

Back on the boat, they had time to study the front page. Nobody could sleep properly anyway. 'NT SET TO BOOM: Exclusive by Felicia Caxton.' There was a five-column wide picture of Hiram in his hotel room, gesturing out across the mud flats of the harbour at low tide, with an empty champagne glass. The picture editor had cropped the photograph, cutting out the table next to Hiram which had shown a bottle of raspberry lemonade and a copy of a business magazine published by a different rich bastard from the one who employed the picture editor. Still, the rest of the photograph was unmistakably Hiram, and the quotes even more so.

When Miranda woke up after fitful dreams about her brains melting and dribbling out of her ear on to the pillow, she ran the cold shower over her head, shook her hair like a labrador on the beach, and went down to fish out the paper. On the way back up the stairs, she unfolded it to the front page and burst out laughing.

'I'll give you a bloody exclusive, lady,' she said, glancing at the clock as she reached for the phone. It was 5 am and she was due on air at six.

'This better be good,' said the voice on the other end of the phone.

'Sorry, boss, you'll have to do breakfast yourself. I've got the story of the year.'

'Christ, Miranda. Why can't you get your scoops at a civilised hour?'

'Just listen, Fingle,' she said. Fingle did. Fingle smiled. And Fingle did the breakfast shift. Miranda drove into work, picked up a recorder and headed for the Plaza. On her way in, she heard the weather report. 'Possible showers.'

'Possible showers nothing,' she said, aloud. 'You've been saying that for three weeks, and the only showers we get are courtesy of the plumbing.' Her mind turned to the job at hand: exposing Hiram, and therefore Franklin, who still hadn't agreed to an interview, even though she'd left several messages with Gavin Baskerville.

'If this doesn't flush Franklin out of the wood-work, nothing will,' she said to herself.

'If he's running for cover on this, he won't want to get into even more trouble. I hope.' She thought of Selina, and braked to avoid being hit by a taxi speeding through a red light, its driver laughing maniacally, with a startled woman and two suit-cases in the back seat. 'Hope you make the early flight, sweetheart,' thought Miranda. 'I think I might do the same when this mess is sorted out.'

At 7 am, Rosie Minjawirra came on duty and woke Jock and Eric with a cup of coffee and the paper.

'Hi,' she said. 'What a class act you two are. Heavy night? Had to sleep it off in the psych ward?'

The two men grumbled, scratched around in their eyeballs and their underpants and said thanks for the coffee. Well, what they both said approximated 'Uuurrghh'.

'Charmed, I'm utterly sure,' said Rosie.

Jock threw his feet over the edge of the couch and looked down at his crumpled suit. 'Poop,' he said.

'Good morning to you, too, Doctor,' said Rosie.

Eric opened his eyes very wide and stared at the ceiling, only his head visible above a white sheet that he clutched around his chin.

He jerked his head around, saw Jock and Rosie, screamed, 'Aaaaaaarghhh!' and put his head underneath the sheet again.

'Most alluring,' said Rosie. 'May I remind you gentlemen that under the Mental Health Act of the Northern Territory, the man on that bed should be brought before a magistrate before 9 pm this evening—no, not you Dr Urbanburger—or he will be discharged. Obviously he can't be discharged in his present state, so I suggest that we arrange a bedside hearing for 7 pm. I will inform Mrs Franklin, and notify the court before the close of business today. Good morning.' Rosie turned and left the room.

'It is bloody not a good bloody morning,' shouted Eric, slightly muffled under the sheet.

'Careful, mate, you'll start sounding Australian in a minute. Wakey, wakey, hands off snaky, rise and shine . . .' said Jock, opening the paper from the back page inwards, to get to the classifieds.

'Oh, shut up,' grizzled Eric, throwing off the sheet.

'Oh, look, our ad's in the paper.'

'Oh, great.'

'Do you think we could stop talking in sentences that start with 'O' now?'

'Oh, nuts.'

'Evidently not. Well, my esteemed colleague, we should hear from that gang of desperadoes any minute now . . .'

The phone rang.

Eric grimaced. 'This is getting worse. Not only are you talking in clichés, but they're coming true. I hate this. I hate this. I hate this . . .' He continued the litany as he got down off the trolley.

Jock picked up the phone. 'Dr Jovanovich,' he said. 'Yep. Uh-huh. Yeah, he's here. We'll be there. Yeah. Have a nice day.' He hung up.

'. . . I hate this. I mean it, I really hate this,' said Eric.

'Effie,' said Franklin in his sleep. 'Effie.'

'We must prepare ourselves for the day's events.'

'Who the hell are you, Shorts, Darth Vader? Get a grip, buddy, we're probably gonna be arrested. Or shot,' said Eric.

Jock idly flipped over the newspaper. 'Holy fuck!'

'Right, that's it. That kinda language is the most unimaginative so far. I can't stand it any more . . .' Jock held up the front page for Eric to see the enormous photograph of Hiram.

'Well I'll be a griddle-warped iguana in Elvis's handbag,' said Eric.

'My point exactly,' replied Jock. 'Although I would have said girdle-wrapped. No matter. Let's get back to the hotel before the Martians arrive.'

184

'What?!'

'Had you going there, didn't I? No, I don't think we need Martians. We've kidnapped a Minister and had him sedated and concealed it from the police, we've—OK, OK, *I've* allowed an indisputably wacko patient to impersonate a millionaire, probably damaging him for life by encouraging his crazy fantasies. How can I convince him he's not a millionaire entrepreneur now? It's in the paper! And the woman I fell in love with is still in the hands of men with small brains, one of whom is a crazed architect.'

'Ah . . . but no Martians?' checked Eric.

'Nup.'

'That's all right then. Let's proceed, at warp thang. I thought you were going to go all Californian on me there for a minute.'

'Ya want me to channel Joan of Arc again?' asked Jock, as they passed the matron's empty desk on the way to the lifts.

'No, Jock. No.'

'Party-pooper. Garçon, garçon, bring me some marshmallows!'

'Oh, Gard. Hey, I was dreaming that I was in *Beach Blanket Bingo*. There was a big party on the sand, and I didn't have any clothes on, and some men in airforce uniforms were stacking up huge packing crates with "Largactyl" stamped on the side. Some wolves tried to speak to me, but I put my fingers in my ears and sang the Mickey Mouse theme song until they ran away. I was drowning, trying to attract attention, but Annette Funicello was surfing, using Frankie Avalon as a board. Then we were on the beach again and she was waxing him with a swede.'

'A Swede?'

'Yeah, one of those little vegetable things. You know, they make soup outta them.'

'That's no way to talk about Stefan Edberg,' Jock said sternly.

'Look, just tell me, what do you think the dream means?'

'Did Frankie Avalon say anything to you?'

'No, but he winked,' said Eric, as they pushed open the hospital entrance doors and headed for the car-park.

'Your dream means that you are going to become the first head of the University of Harvard's Psychiatric Ethics Committee to conduct television interviews in a Hawaiian shirt,' replied Jock.

'Yeah, that's what I thought.'

Lying on a swag on the deck of the *Effie*, Selina stretched and sighed, weighed down already by the oppressive humidity. 'Squeeze me, baby, I am that Wettex,' she sang tunelessly. Another night of virtually no sleep. She shouldered Briian out of the way to take a cold shower and change her T-shirt. She washed the one she had slept in, wrapped the sarong around herself and hung the T-shirt on the deck rail on her way to the thug brigade. They were sitting around the card table under a piece of shade cloth on the stern, looking a bit haggard themselves, not to say grumpy.

'What's the matter, boys?' she said.

'We're supposed to swap you for Franklin tonight,' said Briian.

'I don't know,' said Lefty. 'I've never done anything like this before,' he added.

The others stared at him. 'Well, I bloody haven't,' he said defensively. 'I met the fat bastard in a bar in Hong Kong, where I was trying to get a job on a boat. I don't wanna go back to Sydney 'cos there's a warrant out for me on possession. I got off the shit and took off for Asia. The next thing I know, I'm minding his yacht while the usual skipper is off to Argentina to see his dying uncle or some bloody thing, and the next thing I know after that, I'm some kind of muscle with a gun. That's a three-year-away job. Hell of a way to make a living, but no boss, no pay, so I guess we'd better do the swap.'

The others looked a bit shocked. He'd never said so many words at one time. Especially in sentences.

'There isn't going to be any shooting, is there?' said Briian.

'Not unless people lose it. I don't have a good feeling about that American. And I'm a bit worried about that Doctor Yovvyanyovich or whatever his name is. He seems a bit short of the full quid to me.'

'That's all I need,' thought Selina, her mind racing off in a few directions at once, 'a mad psychiatrist on my side. What's he doing in Darwin? And who's the American? Who wants the Americans on their side? All you get is a whole lot of nuclear-targeted bases and your wheat market shot to buggery.'

'Who is this bloke, anyway?' said Briian. 'Your new boyfriend?'

'Briian,' said Selina, 'You're a dickhead.'

'He is, isn't he?' said Lefty.

Briian retired, miffed, to read a Phantom comic below deck, while Selina dangled her legs over the side of the boat, wearing a big straw sun-hat of Effie's she'd found in a locker. She thought about Jock, and she thought about her parents, and she thought about how things can go very strange very quickly. Mind you, the week had started somewhat prophetically with an eviction, a job loss, getting sawn in half, and possibly falling in love, and was approaching its close with kidnapping, threats against her life, and the man she may be falling in love with landing on the other side of the continent and trying to rescue her from some kind of million dollar zoning law fraud. 'Gee,' she thought, 'I can't wait for the weekend!'

And Jock. It was a hell of a white shining knight act, if white and shiny were what you wanted. On the other hand, perhaps Jock was also involved in the whole shemozzle. After all, he was obviously rich. Maybe he just wanted his ten grand back. 'I always thought money would mean freedom,' Selina mused, staring mournfully at the shore.

She had to admit that even in the midst of this lunacy she was still plagued by crazy, romantic thoughts. Jock Jovanovich. Would he be fun to be around? Would he like kissing? (Of course he'd like kissing, what was she talking about.) Would he be good at it? That was the question. He was obviously a Pants Man, and she hadn't had time to plug into the Melbourne girlie network's data base. She had thought she could wait till she got back to Melbourne before doing the phone reconnaissance. It was a bastard getting to know somebody new anyway. What if he hated *Thelma and Louise*? She slapped a mozzie and it came off second best.

Would her knees go weak when she saw him again, or would her stomach just turn over, like the usual infatuation? Maybe there'd be some completely new biological reaction. Her left elbow might trace a figure eight in the air, or her ears might wriggle shamelessly. Who cared. The important thing was to get away from this mob. 'I've been thinking about *Hornrims of Desire* too much,' she admitted to herself. Falling in love? Flailing in lerv, more like it. Spring is sprung, the grass is riz, I wonder where my boyfriend is? What was the name of that comedian with great ears? Maybe she could give him a call when she went back. Went back? Oh, yeah, that old thing. 'I'm crazed with goofy thoughts when I should be making cunning plans,' she told herself. 'It must be the conditioning of women over centuries by fairy tales, pulp fiction, pop songs, soap operas and the bridal industry. Or the humidity. Who can tell?'

Selina went downstairs, got a bottle of still mineral water out of the fridge and ignored Briian. 'What's wrong with being single for a while anyway?' she asked herself. 'You can eat toast and fart in bed at the same time without fear of recrimination, and you get to sharpen up your flirting skills. You don't lie awake at night next to somebody wondering how on earth you ever got into this for a joke, and you have to make fewer compromises in your life. Still, there's kissing . . .' she thought wistfully, staring out a porthole, or more accurately, through the shards of a porthole.

'Hey, get us a beer out of the fridge would you?' said Briian, not taking his eyes off Diana Palmer, who had gone to the United Nations and left the Phantom baby-sitting Kit and what's-her-name in the Skull Cave. Selina took a red can out of the fridge, shook it vigorously behind the fridge door while she sang a few bars of her favourite Madonna song, 'Express Yourself', put it down carefully in front of Briian, and nicked up the stairs before he reached out slowly, eyes still on the comic, and popped the top.

'OK lads,' said Selina, on deck. 'Who's up for Canasta?'

Miranda was being held up at the Plaza reception by Chloe.

'Come on Chloe, let me just go up and knock on his door.'

'No way, missy, it's not worth my while. Management is on my back. Why don't we just ring Mick Maguire and get Hiram arrested on fraud charges? I'm sick of the lot of them, getting in everyone's way, and those blokes with guns at the yacht club last night were the last straw. Anything could have happened. I'm not convinced that they're helping get Selina back, I think it's time we . . .'

'Chloe, I'm not arguing with you,' interrupted Miranda. 'I think it's time the cops spoke to Jock and Eric too, but I just think we should talk to them first. Anyway, Hiram's as nutty as all get out, they're not going to arrest him. And Chloe, Chloe, listen; if they do, then I can't report anything. Once they lay charges, I can't report any details of the case. It'll be *sub judice*. Let me get to Hiram, try and find Jock and Eric and get a quote out of at least one of them, then I can run the story on radio and get Franklin in a corner. He'll have to . . .'

'Here come the Cowboy Brothers now; they can take you up as a guest,' said Chloe, looking over Miranda's shoulder towards the revolving doors, which had just deposited a couple of extremely dishevelled health professionals on the mock-marble parquetry. 'Go for it.'

Miranda was already half-way to them, tape on, microphone forward. 'Dr Jovanovich, have you seen the paper this morning?'

'Yes, Miss Spurn, I have. It is a matter of great concern to me.'

'I imagine it *is* a matter of some concern to you, sir, that a patient under your care has claimed to be a millionaire entrepreneur and has signed a deal with the Territory Government to provide funding and facilitate the building of a multi-million-dollar tourist development.'

'What was the question?'

'Jo-ock.' Miranda rolled her eyes.

'OK, I'll give it to you straight. You on? You ready? Let's do it.'

Miranda's eyes dropped to check the recording level while Jock was speaking, and then returned to his face again. 'OK go.'

'Hiram F. Doppelganger is a patient of mine. Until this week he was a resident of a permanent-care home for the mentally ill in Melbourne. He is not considered dangerous, and due to funding cuts in the state and federal health budgets, he is one of many people on the streets who could perhaps be better cared for in a community house. But he's not. He is travelling with me because he doesn't know where else to go.'

'So he is under your care.'

'No, but I am sorry that this situation has arisen.'

'Don't you admit responsibility for this appalling state of affairs?'

'No, I don't. Why should I? Nobody has ever believed Hiram before. Four-year-old children can tell he's not a millionaire. Nuns with no experience of the outside world can tell he's not a property developer, but a man with delusions of grandeur.'

'I *love* this! Give me a man who speaks in grabs and give him to me now! YES! Um, hang on Jock . . . OK . . . Dr Jovanovich, do you have any idea how your patient, a fifty-five-year-old mental patient, could have convinced the Deputy Premier and the Government of the Northern Territory that he was a multi-millionaire property developer so that they would sign an agreement with him for a joint venture?'

Jock paused. 'No,' he said. 'No, actually, I've been kind of busy the last couple of days, and Hiram's generally pretty harmless; I mean, he bails people up in the street sometimes and tries to talk to them about share prices, but, you know, people just humour him, I suppose . . .'

'What do you think that says about the Territory Government?'

'I think perhaps they felt an affinity with Mr Doppelganger,' said Jock.

'Nu-uh,' said Miranda, 'Libel. Try again.'

'Um . . . I'm deeply shocked that the Territory Government could have mistaken Mr Doppelganger for a real millionaire. As far as I know he relies on an invalid pension each week. And, I might add, somebody taking him seriously might adversely affect his mental health.'

'Thank you, Dr Jovanovich,' said Miranda, grinning.

'Excu-u-use me,' said Eric, 'but that was the most bogus door-stop interview I've ever seen. You practically told him what to say!'

'Settle,' smiled Miranda. 'Jock, what's the name of the home Hiram was in? And which body of psychiatry are you registered with in Melbourne?'

She wrote down the answers in a spiral-bound notebook. 'OK, once I've checked you out, this goes to air. I don't know whether to run it as an exclusive or hit the Premier with it at the press conference. What do you think?'

'Check him out?' spluttered Eric. 'He's just as much a lunatic as Hiram!'

'Yeah, but he's a doctor. Now, we'll see if this

doesn't flush Franklin out of the woodwork, the bastard. I'm sure he knows where Selina is. You don't, do you, boys?' she arched an eyebrow.

'No,' said Jock truthfully. 'Honest.'

'What was all that fuss last night at the yacht club then? They were the blokes who broke in and took Selina, weren't they?'

'You don't miss a trick, Miranda,' said Jock. 'Yeah. We got in touch with them through the classifieds, but no go. You saw them run off.'

'Well, where did they go?'

'I don't know,' said Jock irritably.

'Then stop being a dork and tell the police what you know. This isn't "Miami Vice", you know,' she said to Eric.

'Oh, thank you very much. Shall I just beat myself over the head with a stone because I was born in America, honey?'

'Don't call me honey, mate.'

'Heeeerarrgh!' said Jock.

'Look, I've gotta go,' said Miranda. 'Sorry Eric. There's going to be a press conference in about an hour. Hopefully Franklin will be there, and we can ask him about Selina. Even getting a denial that he knows anything about it will put the pressure on. After the press conference, I'm going to try and lean on Connie—remember, his secretary? —for some evidence of this zoning law scam. By "PM" tonight, we should have him . . . you know . . .'

'Hog-tied?' suggested Eric.

'That'll do.'

Miranda left.

'It wouldn't help if Franklin was found now,' said Jock. 'I'm handling this. We've got to get the girl.'

'You always get the girl.'

'But right now I have to talk to a loony.'

'You know, for a sleepy outpost with ninety-five per cent humidity, things move pretty fast up here,' said Eric.

Jock pouted. 'I wish my brain would keep up with it.'

'Can I go home now? I'd rather face fifteen FBI agents and a McDonald's hamburger than this. Well, fifteen FBI agents, anyway. Which reminds me . . . I wonder where . . .' They wandered off to the lifts.

The first part of Miranda's plan went well. By ten past nine she had blown Hiram's identity on the radio news (the interstate bulletins had taken the story as more evidence of frontier looniness in the north), erased a tape in a special magnetised cupboard to take to the press conference, and arranged to meet Connie before that.

Inside the government offices, the Premier of the Northern Territory was shouting at Gavin Basker-ville. 'For heaven's sake, man! Franklin is the only one who knows what's going on and he's not here! I thought we were just going to announce an in-principle agreement to inject a few mill into the tourist industry! And now this! Where *is* the bastard?'

'His wife says he's sick, sir.'

'Sick? I don't care if he's been decapitated. Get him in here. What are we going to say at this press conference? Shortly we're going to have to explain why the Government has agreed in principal to let a certified maniac build its biggest ever tourist development!'

'Certified maniac's a bit strong, Premier. I believe that "sanity-challenged" is the current buzz-word.'

The Premier stared at him, amazed. 'Do something, Gavin.'

'Premier, I can only suggest that you say that you don't know anything about it. Deny everything. Say the story's not true . . .'

'It is true, though, isn't it?'

'Yes,' said Gavin Baskerville, 'What's that got to do with it?'

'Just checking . . . go on.'

'Say it isn't true, that you don't know where the story came from, that the Government has never met with Hiram what's-his-name, and that the Deputy Premier couldn't possibly have signed an agreement with him, because he's, oh hell, he's . . .'

'On a trade mission in Mauritius?' suggested the Premier.

'That'll do. When we find him, we'll square him on the story. At least we can put it all on hold now. Nobody's going to get up at the press conference and call you an out and-out-liar.'

Ha.

Liar, Liar, Your Trousers
Are a Significant Fire Hazard

The weather bureau had its cash on the nose of a big storm later in the day, but it was the sixth time in two weeks that the seething populace had been promised an end to the Build-up. The Department of Rural Affairs policy was to follow the weather bureau's advice. Advised of the likelihood of strong winds coming in at about 2 pm, they proceeded to spray the mangroves behind five suburbs with the standard mosquito larvae pesticide. But, as the pilot said later at the inquiry, 'Whoopsy-narna.' No wind, triple-strength pesticide because Barry was on a bender, and before you know it there are thirty kinder kids in casualty, two pensioners in intensive care and instant death for two thousand six hundred assorted birds.

The air above Darwin became a stranger soup,

pesticides mixed with Kakadu ash and the black, oily smoke from some confiscated Indonesian fishing boats torched by the authorities near the wharves. Half an hour later there was a maniac in the mall with a hatchet, bringing new forms of persuasion to the art of busking, and requiring a couple of bullets in his left leg to slow him up. It was rumoured that the third rendition of 'Jingle Bells' on the mall speakers, and in particular the line 'Dashing through the snow', had brought it on. Before he was apprehended (shot), he managed to take out most of the council's jumbo tinsel collection and make a couple of American tourists feel right at home.

Out in Kakadu, where it was invariably hotter than Darwin, the mostly non-Aboriginal mining town of Jabiru sweltered and svelted. Down at the uranium mine, the power went off for ten minutes, and the emergency generator failed to crank up for the first five. The tailings dam oozed dead, silent water—no birds, no animals. Around it, the cyclone-wire fence shone in the harsh light. 'Typical,' said Seedpod, as she climbed over it. 'I come all the way out here in the heat to make a personal protest, and I have to climb a fence to get a drink.' Thirty seconds after she dropped on to the inside, the electricity surged through the wire again. Seedpod decided to go for a walk around the lake.

Back in town, her composer boyfriend, driven wild by the heat, smoked three joints, lay on the kitchen floor, and put his head in the crisper section of the fridge while he played somebody else's riff on his piano accordion (although he called it sampling). He was the only person at Darwin Hospital by that evening with 'Hypothermia' on his chart.

The weather bureau started getting a little antsy in the afternoon. There seemed to be a storm coming out of nowhere, and if it hit Darwin, they could officially kiss the Build-up goodbye, or more likely, piss off and don't show your face around here for a good while. There was some major turmoil going on in the sky, and the bureau decided that a warning would have to go out, just in case. All emergency services and boats were informed, all radio and TV stations started broadcasting a big storm warning, preceded and punctuated by the magic words, 'This is not a cyclone warning'.

'A big blow on the way,' said Effie, as she hoovered the Twisties off the floor, hurled her husband's toupée off the balcony and turned to look across the harbour—'but not until late afternoon, I reckon.'

By midday, three television crews were in Hiram's hotel room, offering him money to admit he was an invalid pensioner. Hiram was sticking to his story, though, and trying to bluff his way through. The TV shows didn't care if he owned up or not. Either way it was a helluva story. 'Abreast of the News' had offered him $5000 to tell his story, and he was secretly considering it.

It was in this atmosphere that the Premier came into the press conference, which had been deferred because of the events of the day, striding confidently, with a fistful of paper with lies on it. Firstly, he answered questions about the aerial spraying: no danger to the public, obviously of major concern to the Government, committee will be appointed to deliberate on the terms of reference for an inquiry. The *Territory Voice* reporter was satisfied, the ABC tried to get tough, but Felicia Caxton turned the focus to Hiram.

'Premier,' she began, 'Yoo-hoo!'

The Premier turned quickly and smiled. 'I see the chief political commentator wishes to ask a question,' he beamed. She simpered back, eager to rescue him.

'Premier, would you care to comment on the magnificent new development by your Government and Mr Hiram Doppelganger?' The Premier's jaw dropped. He looked at Gavin Baskerville. Baskerville hit himself on the head. He'd forgotten to tell Felicia about Miranda's revelations. Felicia never listened to the ABC. She said it was 'socialist state radio', and frequently editorialised that the annual budget of the ABC was almost precisely the amount that would be required to build the Alice Springs to Darwin railway line, and what could be clearer in terms of priority?

'Yes, sir,' Miranda added, waving her notebook. 'It was revealed this morning that Mr Doppelganger is in fact an invalid pensioner recently released from a residential mental care facility in Melbourne. Sir, why has your Government signed an in-principle agreement to build a multi-million-dollar development with this man?'

'. . .' said Felicia.

The Premier put his hands under the desk, and

looked Miranda straight in the eye. 'Miss Spawn,' he said, deliberately mispronouncing her name, 'I can assure you that the Government has absolutely no knowledge of this story, or where it came from.'

Miranda pursued him. 'Sir, I believe the agreement in-principle was signed by your Deputy Premier, the Zoning Minister and Mr Doppelganger two days ago. Can you comment?'

The Premier licked his lips.

'Mr Franklin is in, er, Khartoum on a trade mission, and we have been in contact with him. No such document exists.'

'Excuse me, Premier,' Felicia interrupted, very confused, 'but I . . . Mr Doppelganger believes that the deal is signed, sealed, and will be formally delivered tomorrow. I spoke to him only last night. I don't understand . . .'

'Well, Felicia,' chuckled the Premier, 'I believe that you have been the victim of this person's over-active imagination. I'm sorry you were taken for a ride, but really, we cannot be blamed!' He spread his hands wide, as if to encompass all the journalists present, as if to enlist them on the side of People Who Can Recognise A Loony When They See One.

Felicia was having none of it. Never had her beloved Government turned against her. Sure, sometimes they asked her to tone it down, but after all the leaks she'd run for them in the past: she'd been betrayed. 'Then why was the story leaked to me by the Zoning Minister's press secretary?!' she said loudly.

Droplets from Gavin Baskerville's forehead started to run down between his eyes and off the end of his nose. It was going to look good on the news. Suddenly this had become a rivetting press conference. There was an unusual spark in the reporters and the camera crews as they scented blood. The slow season had suddenly been fast-forwarded.

The Premier stood up to leave, folding his bits of paper and putting them in his breast pocket. 'I assure you the Government knows nothing of this,' he said smoothly, and strode to the door in what he thought was a manly, in-control fashion, but actually looked like he had a Besser brick up his bum. Gavin Baskerville followed. There was the usual media melée: print reporters were smacked in the head by camera operators who wanted a clear view, radio reporters ran to grab their recorders and microphones from the Premier's desk and rush after him, photographers kicked each other and muttered, 'Sorry, mate' and the sound people told them to shut up.

Reporters howled questions. 'No more,' smiled the Premier, over shouts of 'Where's Mr Franklin?' 'What's he doing in Khartoum?' 'Where *is* Khartoum?' 'We've just heard that a pensioner has been admitted to hospital with breathing problems following the pesticide spraying, sir, can you comment?' And above the clamour, a hard, arresting query from Miranda.

'Premier! What if I could produce the document signed by Mr Franklin and Mr Doppelganger?' Something in her tone, not to mention her question, silenced the others.

The Premier glanced at Gavin Baskerville, who

shook his head slightly and licked his lips. 'There is no such document,' said the Premier. 'I'm sick of you ABC lot trying to stir up trouble.'

'It has long been my ambition to say this at a press conference, Premier,' said Miranda. 'Liar, liar, your pants are on fire.' She produced the document and waved it in his face. 'Here it is, sir, signed by the Deputy Premier. Where is he? Can you comment on this?' She pointed her microphone at him.

The Premier gaped at her. He grabbed the document, and stared at it. Then he glared at Gavin Baskerville. Channel Seven's stringer grabbed the document from him and filmed it, and the *Territory Voice* photographer got a shot of it as well, just in time. Gavin Baskerville lunged forward, snatched it and stuffed the whole page in his mouth. It made fantastic pictures. Poor radio-girl Miranda, but she didn't do too badly, just put on her foreign corres-pondent 'I-am-sitting-on-top-of-a-tank-storming-the-gates-of-the-palace' voice and said, 'The Premier's adviser, Mr Gavin Baskerville is now attempting to eat the document.'

'Jesus!' said the Premier, as he strode out of the room and scurried into the lift. As soon as the doors closed, he started hitting his forehead on the wall.

The reporters, jubilant, adrenalin pumping with the certainty of a great story, compared quotes, and agreed to swap photographs. Scoops were one thing, but everybody had this one, and reporters in Darwin needed to help each other sometimes. It was a favour for favour system, and Miranda gained a few credits by handing out photocopies of the document.

The reporters piled out of the room, heading for phones, dark-rooms and editing suites. Miranda was last, thoughtful. Where *was* Franklin? She was sure that was the key to finding Selina. Even Connie didn't have any idea. Just then she saw Connie come out of the lifts with a group of senior minister-ial advisers who were ignoring her and talking urgently among themselves.

'Hello, Connie,' said Miranda brightly. 'I haven't seen you for ages! Where's the Deputy Premier? I need a quote!'

'I've told you before, Miss Spurn,' said Connie. 'You'll get no information from me. And even though I don't work for the Deputy Premier any more, you never will!'

'Have you been transferred, then?' asked Miranda.

'No, I'm going to Newcastle for a few days. My aunt is very sick. I may not be back for some time,' said Connie carefully.

'You're leaving today, then?' asked Miranda casually.

'I thought that would be best, yeah,' Connie slid her eyes towards the suits, 'if it's all the same to you, *Miss* Spurn.'

'Well, despite our differences, I wish you all the best,' said Miranda.

'Yeah, right,' said Connie. She turned her back to the suits, and gave Miranda a huge wink. Miranda shot out a hand and grasped Connie's arm tightly for a split second. Then she was gone, through the foyer and walking quickly towards the ABC building.

By five o'clock, the national network would be broadcasting her story, live. And she had something up her sleeve. Connie had also given her some stuff from Franklin's own files which he kept in the office: the plans for the development, and a copy of Franklin's title to the land. She hoped she could get a decent comment out of the opposition; most of the time they fought like flummery.

Jock and Eric heard the report on the way to the hospital to pick up Mr Franklin. 'Goddam,' said Eric.

'Wow,' said Jock.

'No,' said Rosie, when she walked in on them getting Franklin out of bed. 'You cannot take Mr Franklin from the hospital without his wife's permission. He's not sedated any more, he could go berserk again at any time. Do you hear me? Out of the question.'

'Matron,' said Jock desperately. 'This is a matter of life or death! We need to get this bastard out of here. Trust me!'

Rosie looked into his eyes. 'I wouldn't trust you if you had a couple of fluffy wings, a halo and a dirty great harp. But that's the first time you've been anywhere near honest with me. I don't know what's going on, and it's been a long day. I've got one more hour of this killer shift. Between now and then, I'm going to do my rounds and some paperwork. I'll pop my head in before I go, OK?'

Jock met her gaze, 'That will do nicely. Thank you, Matron,' he said.

Outside, in the real world, everything went extra quiet. The bats, ants and dogs of Darwin grew reticent, and across the harbour the sky started to take on a dark tinge near the horizon. 'Right on time,' said the duty meteorologist. 'Sunset storm, coming up.' He got on the phone and strengthened the wind warnings to be broadcast.

The captain of the cruise ship *Bonkerama*, moored at the main wharf, glared at the barometer in the command centre. 'Shit,' he said. 'We'll make a run for it anyway. It's not so bad.'

'So we'll stick to plan, skipper? Sailing in an hour?'

'Nothing could deter me, except a cyclone,' confirmed the captain.

'We'll be right then, sir. No chance of a cyclone. Just a little old tropical storm. Those passengers are cutting it a bit fine though,' added the sailor.

'Gringos,' said the captain. 'Shopping, and drinking. They don't mix.'

'We can't sail without them,' said the sailor.

'No, but I'd like to get out of this shit weather. The hombres below deck are sweating like pigs. What a job.' The captain scammed the wharf and, a hundred metres away across a small inlet, the dirt car-park. 'And what a dump . . . they'll be here.'

Next to the car park was a B52 bomber mounted on a huge slab of concrete. The plaque said it had been a gift of the US Army, which, as Miranda once said, is a bit like Vlad the Impaler giving away a couple of old pointy sticks.

At about 6 pm, with a breeze stirring slightly

in the trees, Jock and Eric pulled up to one side of the B52 in a rented Holden. Eric was driving, Jock in the passenger's seat with Rolf at his feet, and Hiram and Franklin in the back. Hiram was holding Franklin's clothes on his lap. Franklin looked like a pile of nylon curtains from the Plaza hotel, because that's what they had stacked on top of him to draw attention from the fact that the car might contain a 24 stone, naked Deputy Premier wanted for questioning and the tendering of voluntary resignations or else.

There was nobody else around. The big, white cruise ship loomed on the other side of the wharf. It was just possible to make out people on the deck.

'I've got the feeling that this is going to be very tricky,' said Eric.

'Wuf,' said Rolf.

A red four-wheel drive pulled in the other entrance to the car-park and stopped opposite, only three car lengths away. In it were three men with guns, Briian, and Selina.

'What am I supposed to do, flash my lights?' asked Eric. 'Sing a couple of verses from "Sound of Music"? Send out for javelins?'

'I don't know,' said Jock. 'Why don't we all just get out of the car?'

'I don't know, let me guess. Because they might shoot us, Jock?' suggested Eric.

'Look, I'm not sure that I like this, lads,' said Hiram. 'I only wanted to get involved in some take-over deals. I'm not used to the rough stuff.'

'Oh, get a grip on yourself,' snapped Eric.

'Steady on,' said Jock. 'OK, we might as well

get on with it. Everybody ready? Right . . . abracadabra!'

A head that had often been compared to a hat full of arse-holes only twice as mean bobbed up from underneath the nylon, and Harold Franklin asked what the bloody hell anybody thought was bloody going on if any bloody body didn't bloody mind bloody telling him.

'We're about to swap you for the young woman you've been holding against her will, Mr Franklin. You remember Mr Doppelganger, I'm sure? He is a mental patient of mine, and there is now a major scandal in your Government over the fact that you', he took a deep breath, 'have signed an agreement with him for this development. Now, I understand that you must sign a bill of sale by midnight so as to make a lot of money. Please behave yourself until we have swapped you for our friend and then you're free to do what you want.'

'Huh?' said Franklin.

'Put your clothes on,' suggested Eric.

'Oh, yeah, right,' said Franklin. The four men got out of the car. When the doors slammed, Jock was reminded briefly of old cop shows, and momentarily, wildly, wished they were all wearing hats. 'Division Four: Leonard Teale would know what to do,' he said.

'He was in "Homicide",' said Hiram.

Franklin stood at the back of the car, trying to get into his strides and put his shirt on at the same time. He had at least cottoned on to the fact that he was on the wrong side of the car-park when it came to allies, and was trying to sidle, which is to say waddle, towards the red car. Jock shook his right hand away from his body as if dislodging some water and said 'Rorschach'. Rolf promptly nipped Franklin on the heels, and then stood in front of him, snarling.

'All right!' said Franklin.

Jock crossed his fingers on both hands and Rolf lay down, ready to guard Franklin until Jock told him otherwise.

The doors of the four-wheel drive opened, and Selina got out first. Lefty followed, holding on to her arm. Briian and the two others got out, and the two groups stared at each other for a moment.

Selina, one hand holding her hat-box, yanked her arm away from Lefty and brushed the hair from her eyes. She looked at Jock. He looked at her. She didn't go weak at the knees, she just felt scared. Lefty grabbed her arm again, and both groups shuffled forward, until they were only a few feet apart. Selina kept looking at Jock, for some sign that she could help with his plan, whatever it was.

Up close, she had an unwelcome and accurate intuition: he didn't *have* a plan. She looked from him to the stranger beside him.

'Hi,' he said.

'Oh, sorry,' said Jock. 'Eric, Selina. Selina, Eric.'

'Let's get this done properly,' said Lefty, 'without any accidents.' The wind was picking up, and most of the sky behind them was a mass of indigo clouds. The sun was going down on the other side of town, and a few big, heavy raindrops fell on to the earth and turned to steam.

Selina edged forward. So did Franklin. They were

almost across to either group when the storm hit, blowing Selina's hair around her face like seaweed. The rain began to fall steadily, but not yet heavily. Darwin, and everything in it that could, drew a big, deep breath of relief, smelling wet dirt and feeling the cool wind rush in.

Suddenly, almost right above their heads, there was a flash, and an extraordinarily large thunderclap. The sky had gone almost black, and three street lights snapped on at the end of the car-park. More terrific noise accompanied several wild, jagged forks of lightning, flung sideways across the sky. Harold Franklin was the only one who had ever seen anything like it before. Then a bolt of lightning struck the B52. Arcs of crackling iridescent blue snaked around the metal against the dark orange of the sunset.

Jock screamed, Rolf bolted into the bushes, Eric grabbed Selina and Selina swore. Hiram went a bit stiff and started walking down the pier to the cruise ship. Franklin ran behind the thugs, two of whom had drawn their guns the moment the sky exploded with noise and brilliantly lit up the car-park. The rain pelted.

The lightning speared through the sky again, showing everyone in exaggerated, frozen moments. Only Hiram was moving, bumbling along the pier. 'Let him go, grab the others!' shouted Franklin. The thugs hesitated. Not more kidnapping! It had been hard enough with the girl, but two blokes as well? 'If they don't come with you, shoot the bastards!' said Franklin. The rain came down like a solid mass of water.

'Are you crazy?' shouted Lefty. 'I'm not murdering anyone!'

Franklin lost it, and started screaming: 'If I tell you to shoot, you'll bloody shoot, you little . . .'

He was interrupted by the sound of laughter and chatter from the other side of the bushes. American voices were singing 'New York, New York'. Franklin glanced in the direction of the noise, and then at the big ship, sparkling white now against the dark sky.

'Hurry up! Get 'em in the car before we're seen!' he yelled. The thugs didn't move.

Franklin took a huge roll of hundred-dollar notes from his suit pocket and shook it at them. 'There's fifteen thousand in it for you, and anything you want later!'

Eric looked at Jock. 'You didn't search his *pockets*? Sheesh!'

'Call it an oversight,' shrugged Jock.

'Give me the bloody gun,' said Franklin, wrenching one from Ken's hand. He pointed it at Jock. 'I've had enough of you.'

Selina threw her voice behind the red car. 'We have the car-park surrounded. Lie down on your faces or we'll pump you full of . . . um, you know . . . lead.' It wasn't entirely convincing, but it was enough to distract everyone's attention for a second, long enough for a jolly band of polyester-clad consumers to come laughing around the corner, clutching shopping bags and cameras, and slightly under the influence of bourbon. A group of very wet, very rich Americans splashed through the car-park, now mud, slapping each other's backs

211

and shoulders and shouting cultural expressions of high regard.

'Hey,' said one, 'ain't you the TV shrink, buddy?'

Eric ran. Rolf bounded through the mud to guard Franklin again, with an apologetic look at Jock. Jock waggled an elbow at him, and made a strange shape with his hands that nobody else noticed. The thugs put their guns under their coats, Selina and Jock yelled 'Serendipity!' together and looked at each other in amazement as Franklin started taking his clothes off again.

'Oh, that is *gross*,' said one of the Americans, hurrying past.

'Yes, isn't it,' said Jock in his best, poncey, Roger Moore voice, as he grabbed Selina's hand and propelled her along with him, and the tourists, towards the ship. 'Time we were all getting back, anyway, isn't it?'

'Yeah, I guess so,' said Cubby from Illinois. 'Put it there buddy: you must be from C deck. That TV shrink sure is shy.'

'After a fashion,' said Jock.

Selina's head was spinning, but she did know that behind her were three men with guns and that ahead of her looked pretty attractive, option-wise. 'How's Miranda?' she said.

'OK. Fine. Really. Where has Hiram got to?' said Jock, beside her.

'Who?' said Selina.

The rain was letting up, and the ship's siren gave a long, low honk. Half an hour before departure, as Cubby explained. The captain appeared as the bedraggled passengers were coming up the gang-

212

way. 'You almost missed the boat,' he said. 'Come aboard, ladies and gentlemen.' He turned to an officer nearby, who was looking at Selina and Jock.

'Is that all?'

'Yes, sir, but . . .

'Oh, but me no thingies, my friend, let's get this boat on the river,' he said, striding away and up the stairs towards the bridge. Jock and Selina stood on the deck, still holding hands, soaked to the skin, and fairly rattled, as the officer approached them.

'What are you doing here?' he said.

'Hiram!' said Jock, astonished.

'You must be mistaken, sir. My name is Franciscus Cous-Cous, and I am the personnel officer on the ship. And you, I believe, are stowaways! Captain!' he called up the stairs. 'Stowaways!'

The captain was down the stairs in a flash. 'Get off my beautiful ship!' he said.

'We can't,' said Selina, looking back towards the car-park, the thugs and their red car.

'Piss off,' Jock muttered to them under his breath.

The captain was furious. 'How did this happen? You're new aren't you?' he peered at Hiram. 'Call the police. No, don't call the police, it will hold us up; don't contact the police under any circumstances. We'll just kick them off,' he said, turning his attention to the couple. Hiram wandered off.

'Just a moment of your time, sir, if I may,' said Jock. 'My fiancé and I,' he winced as Selina kicked him hard in the shin, 'are desirous of getting married, and we'd like to have it done on a ship. It's so romantic. I believe you may have to delay the ship another half an hour in any case, so why don't you marry us, sir, and help to make this a joyous occasion . . .' Jock took the captain's hand, jerking it up and down rapidly. 'That's splendid of you, sir, now if we could just assemble some passengers as witnesses, you can have a public-relations coup on your hands, and we'll be out of your hair and on our way.'

'Stay here,' said the captain. 'I'll just go and get a bible and some witnesses.'

'I don't believe this,' said Selina. 'What the fuck are you doing?'

'Well, do you want to go back down there?'

'No, but why don't you just tell him what's happened . . . this is ridiculous!'.

'Because if he calls the police, then they're going to find out that I've broken about six laws and will have to be struck off. Also, it just buys us some time.'

'What? Why are you talking in clichés? What do we need time for?'

'Maybe we should get married anyway.'

'*What*?!'

'Why not?'

'Oh, God. Because its ludicrous. Because I don't even know you. I met you, what, seven days ago. Because marriage is an unnecessary institution, or maybe it isn't, it's just a piece of paper, it's meaningless as an expression of love or possibly a beautiful commitment, but look, could we discuss this philosophical point another time, perhaps?'

'There you go, it's meaningless, so we'll just get divorced in a couple of days.'

'Don't we have to have blood tests, and stuff?

Listen, if this is about the money, you can have it back.'

'It's not about the money. Just trust me,' he gave her a pathetic puppy-dog look. 'You don't need the blood tests and stuff on a ship. Ah . . . Captain, you're ready, splendid. Darling? We can use my mood ring.'

'Fuck off.'

13

Warm and Wet

Chloe had been roped in to help supervise the cocktail waiters for the government's drinks at the Plaza. By dusk, several party faithful had found their way to the foyer, not least to gossip and speculate on the Premier's position. Several were late, having stayed at home to watch the fiasco on the TV news. It was too late to cancel. The Premier and his advisers had decided to brazen it out, although frantic efforts were being made behind the scenes to locate Franklin. So far, they had tracked him to the hospital on information from his wife, only to find that two unknown psychiatrists had checked him out. It was unclear whether he'd been a voluntary or involuntary patient.

'Something else to keep quiet,' thought the

Premier, as he entered the Plaza and began his greetings. He looked at faces closely: not too many eyes failed to hold his. He concluded that his position was safe for the moment ... but precarious. Franklin would have to resign of course, but that would be all right—he could be reappointed later, or given a cushy job with lots of travel. Wouldn't do to upset him too much. Not only did he know which skeletons were in the party cupboards, he was on speaking terms with every vertebra.

Miranda was doing a live-to-air interview with one of the nuns at Hiram's former nursing home when her producer waved from the other side of the studio glass and pointed to a bedraggled Eric, who had just come in, short of breath and long on stories. Miranda beckoned them in as she thanked Sister Mary-Louise.

The producer ushered him into a chair in the studio and dropped some headphones on him. Miranda picked up the computer's playlist, randomly chosen from fifteen hundred easy-listening hits, threw it over her shoulder, put on Lou Reed, and got some preliminary details out of Eric. She also made a quick phone call to Mick Maguire.

The song finished, and she hit the 'On Air' button. 'This is Miranda Spurn, back with the special extended afternoon show from Darwin,' she said. 'It's just gone 6.46 pm, and Barry Ralph will be reporting on those pesticide cases in the seven o'clock news. It has been an extraordinary news day, of course, for the start of the Wet, not least because of the revelations concerning Mr Harold Franklin, the Deputy Premier. The ABC has uncovered startling new aspects to the case, but first, some background.

'Mr Franklin appears to have signed an agreement to build a multi-million-dollar tourist resort with an invalid pensioner, apparently under the impression that the man, recently released from an institution in Melbourne, was a millionaire property developer. It is alleged that recent changes announced to the zoning laws by Mr Franklin will result in the Minister himself making millions of dollars from land in the Darwin area. We would like to have Mr Franklin himself answer these questions, but he has not been available to the media for two days now. He failed to deliver the Mining Industry Council's keynote address at its conference last night. His speech, 'Soil Erosion is Just God's Way of Getting Us Closer to the Goodies', was delivered by the Minister for Tourism, Mr Blain. There is intense speculation about Mr Franklin's whereabouts. The Premier is under heavy pressure, of course, but is denying that his Government knew anything of the deal. It seems that when Mr Franklin does return, he'll be out on a limb. The Party faithful have gathered at the Plaza Hotel tonight for what was going to be a fund-raising cocktail party. The opposition is calling it a wake. In the studio with me now is a visiting American psychiatrist, Dr Eric Urbanburger, who claims to have seen Mr Franklin in the last hour. Dr Urbanburger, what state was the Minister in?'

'Natural, I guess you'd call it,' drawled Eric.

'Excuse me?'

'Buck naked, Miss Spurn. Walking along the wharf road from the car-park.'

'Are you sure it was the Deputy Premier?'

'Yep.'

'Do you know where he was going?'

'No ma'am, I don't.'

'Did you try to speak with him?'

'No, ma'am, he was accompanied by a cattle dog and three men who were waving guns around and picking up money outta the mud. I felt it in-advisable to approach.'

'Did the men appear to be threatening the Minister at all?'

'No, Miss Spurn, I believe they appeared to be on cordial terms. They seemed to be tryin' to get him back into his trousers.'

'And we understand that the police are on their way to investigate these startling revelations. Thank you, Dr Urbanburger . . . One can only wonder what is going through the mind of the Premier, being briefed of these extraordinary developments down at the Plaza Hotel.'

'Incidentally, little lady . . .' began Eric.

Miranda coughed. 'Yes, Dr Urbanburger?'

'I believe they're serving free drinks down there,' he said.

'News coming up, after this song,' said Miranda, who pushed two buttons, took off her headphones and handed them to Barry Ralph. 'Let's go find them, Eric. I won't feel good about Selina until I can see her myself.'

'We'll meet them at the Plaza, I'm sure. As soon as the cops pick up the gun-guys, there'll be nothing between them and us.'

'Why were you talking in a Texas accent?'

'It's this place. It just . . .'

'Yeah, I know.'

There had been a small disagreement when Selina could not be persuaded to accept Jock's mood ring, but compromised with part of the key-ring of the red four-wheel drive. The bridegroom had hissed, 'No wonder they're still there, you idiot!' and the bride's response had been surprisingly inventive. Finally, it was almost over.

'Oh, all right, I will, and then let's get out of here,' said Selina crossly.

'Then I pronounce you husband and wife,' said the Captain. 'You may kiss the bride.'

'No he may not,' Selina snapped. 'Come on, let's go! I've got to find Miranda, and probably help to get that mob locked up.' She looked across to the car-park as Cubby and his wife Candy threw rice on her, much of which stuck in her hair.

A few passengers waved them goodbye as the

muddy couple cantered down the gangway to the wharf. The personnel officer came down to farewell them, and the captain went up to the bridge to supervise the cast-off. 'I think you'd better come with us,' said Jock gently.

'I'll be all right,' said Hiram winking. 'As James Thurber said, "You can fool too many people too much of the time". It's been fun. See ya sometime,' he said, saluted smartly and then marched back up to the ship.

Jock shook his head, and then laughed out loud. Selina pushed him. 'Snap out of it, Kildare, for heaven's sake.' They started to walk down the gangway, still holding hands. Selina had allowed him to carry her hat-box after a short discussion about how it had nothing to do with feminism.

Across the wharf at the car-park, three men with bulging pockets and a coat-hanger were trying to break into the four-wheel drive as Constable Djambin and his colleague pulled up in a police car.

'I hate to say this, but, Oy, oy, oy, what's all this then?' he said. Apart from anything else, it was Constable Djambin's promotion, and he knew it. And a much nicer way of getting one than slaving over a few verbals, too. 'Hands on the top of the car, and don't move until we've got you disarmed,' he said. 'Are you aware of your rights under Australian law? You are being charged . . . '

'Christ,' said Lefty, 'It's our car!'

' . . . with kidnapping and assault for a start. Move.'

Five minutes later, the three men sat handcuffed in the back of the patrol car, and Constable Djambin

221

was talking into the radio as Selina and Jock came off the pier and across the car-park.

'Are you Miss Plankton?' he asked, interrupting himself.

'Yep.'

'Are these the men who kidnapped you?'

She looked into the back of the cop car. 'Ah, yeah. Sorry Lefty.'

'Me too.'

They shook hands as best they could.

Constable Djambin spoke into the microphone again. 'Got a make from the victim. Notify all stations and units she's been found, yeah? OK.' He hung up the microphone. 'Wanna come and make a statement now, Miss Plankton?'

'Nup. The bloke with the moustache assaulted my friend Miranda. Try and find him a cell with a serial killer will you?'

'You OK? You wanna go to the hospital? Did they hurt you, or . . .'

'No, I don't need to go to the hospital. I want some sleep. I'll give you a statement in the morning.'

'OK, that'll do. Where will you be?'

'At my friend Miranda's place.'

'I know it. I think you'll find her at the Plaza with all the other journos. About the statement, I'll come and get you about nine, OK? You all right with this bloke?' He looked dubiously at Jock.

'Yeah, he's OK.'

'Sorry we can't give you a lift.'

'Can I use the red car?'

'Whose is it?'

'Theirs.'

'If anyone found out it would be a bit unethical,' he said, and drove away.

Selina opened the red car, tossed the keys to Jock, and he started the car. 'The Plaza, madam?'

'Mmm,' she said, sprawling in the seat. 'I've had a rough week. You?'

'Same,' he said, smiling.

'Thought so. So, what's been happening?'

Jock laughed again, reached over and stroked her cheek. 'You'd better ask Miranda, she'll explain it all better than me. I'm just glad you're OK. I'm better than glad you're OK.'

It took them a while to push through the journalists and people after a free drink, who were laying siege to the Plaza and get through to the foyer door. Miranda, eyes shining and clutching a tape recorder, was at the door with Eric. She and Selina leaped at each other, holding each other in a bear hug. Eric and Jock also embraced.

'Let's go in,' said Jock. 'We're staying here, after all. You can be our guest, Miranda.'

'They won't let any media in,' she said.

'Oh, for God's sake,' said Eric. 'Hey, all you media people! I'm a guest at this hotel. Here's my key!' He held it up. 'You're all invited inside! Especially you,' he added in an aside to an *Independent* reporter wearing Elvis earrings.

He stepped inside, and the camera crews, reporters and photographers surged in behind him. Across at the bar, Gavin Baskerville looked vacantly at the milling hordes searching for him and the Premier. He tried to be positive—they'd weathered scandals before. Somehow the electorate forgave them, or didn't care. There was a puritanical streak in Territorians, and as long as the allegations weren't about sex, things would be jake.

The Premier was patting Effie Franklin on the arm, and saying that Harold would be looked after as soon as he was located, but that until then, she should keep quiet about the nature of his disappearance, for everybody's sake. She was thinking about divorce.

There was a commotion from the back of the media pack. They parted, stepping back and swinging their lights and cameras around as Harold Franklin came through the revolving door in the nuddy, herded by a wet and panting blue heeler.

The whole crowd, party faithful, crews, reporters, public servants and hotel staff gasped—it was hard to imagine there could be any air left in the foyer, really. In the split second of silence, Selina breathed the magic word: 'Abracadabra'.

Franklin snapped awake, and realised that he was in front of all his colleagues and a significant number of TV cameras without his clothes on. It was too much for him. As the first pangs of the coronary began, he lurched towards his wife. Like many in their last moments, he had an eye on redemption. 'Darling!' he cried, but lunged forward and clutched the Premier instead, a result of blurred vision. 'I can explain everything, my one, my only love!' he shouted into the Premier's face, and dropped dead.

'Damn,' groaned Miranda. 'Now I'll have to stay up for hours getting something on this for "AM".'

Jock opened the door of the room with his over-sized, Hotel-Guests-Are-So-Moronic-They'd-Lose-A-Key-If-It-Didn't-Weigh-More-Than-An-Average-Toddler room key. He looked up in time to see Eric and the *Independent* reporter destined for a little lie down in Eric's room. Eric winked. Jock grinned and held open his door. Selina went in first, dumping her hat-box just inside the door. He came in after her, threw the key on top of the shelf above the mini-bar, dislodging several packets of vastly over-priced peanuts.

He swapped the sign on the door-handle from 'Please Make Up My Room' to 'Do Not Disturb'. He put the chain on. Then he fell backwards on to the king-sized bed and lay looking at the ceiling. Selina crawled up from the end of the bed, lay on her belly and propped her chin in her hands.

'I won't stay long,' she said. 'I just don't want to go back to the house while Miranda's working. I'll go home with Chloe.'

He reached up slowly, eyes locked on hers, and gently ran his knuckles down the line of her cheek. He smoothed some hair away from her forehead, and smiled as a ringlet rebelled and there was a shower of rice. He put his hand on the back of her head, drew it down gently, and kissed her square on the nose.

'Thanks,' he said quietly.

'What?'

'You saved me from getting shot in the car-park.'

'You came looking for me.'

'Yeah. I was going to rescue you, with noble deeds and irresistible hunkiness.'

'Hunkiness?'

'Machismo.'

'Gezundheit.'

'What?'

'Just a bad joke. Never mind. So, Kildare, what *did* you do, out of interest?'

'Well,' said Jock, 'I lied, and cheated, and mislaid a patient, and nearly got my head blown off, and I kidnapped a Minister of the Crown and no doubt contributed to his death by heart attack. I'm pretty sure I'm going to give up psychiatry.'

'What will you do?'

'Bet on horses. That's how I make most of my money anyway. So, are you OK?'

'Mmmm. I was scared, though. You know the scariest thing?'

'Guns.'

'No. I mean, yes, they were scary. But the worst part of it is that they nearly got away with it all, and only three of them will get into any trouble. I mean, Franklin's dead, and whoever else knows about it won't even be found out, probably. Except Briian. And come to think of it, he'd dob anybody in if it meant an easy time for himself. But they nearly all made a packet, and I thought they were going to kill me.'

'It's all over now.'

'It is not all over. The big boys have got money. They can buy friends. They can certainly buy lawyers. The muscle boys will get in the most trouble for having guns and for kidnapping me, but the real bastards get off, or maybe they're up on corporate fraud. They don't put you away for very long for fraud do they?' she asked. 'And the whole mob of them that sees back-room deals as the way to the top . . . Miranda's right—The Crocodile Club.'

She came off her elbows and rolled into Jock's side, her head on his shoulder, one hand on his chest. They were quiet.

After a while, Selina said, 'This is a horrible shirt.'

While Jock was laughing, the phone rang. He reached out his free hand and picked it up. 'Hi, Chloe. No, that's OK. Yeah. Put them through. Hello? Yep, yeah. Nothing to do with me really, I think I got in the way. Not a scratch on her. I'll tell her, but I think she knows. I'll get her to ring you in the morning. Goodnight to you, too.'

He hung up and looked down his nose at Selina. 'That was your mum. She says they love you.'

'Pardon me, since when do you have conversations with my mother while I'm in the room, and I don't even get to know she's on the phone?'

'Hey, she said she would talk to you tomorrow. She said she wants you to get some sleep. Anyway, never you mind,' he said smugly. 'They like me. I should have told them we're on our honeymoon. I reckon they fancy me as a son-in-law. Which side of the bed do you want, Mrs Jovanovich?'

Selina groaned. 'I'd forgotten about that.' She

unfolded herself, leaned against the wall, and narrowed her eyes.

'Uh-oh,' he said.

'Before you get ready to carve another notch in that artisan's dream of a belt, Doctor, I have to tell you something.'

'I know, I'm dangerously handsome and you won't be able to keep your hands off me . . .'

'You may have a surfeit of boyish charm, but I once promised Miranda and Ky I'd never sleep with a married man. Also, most particularly, never sleep with anybody on the first date.' Selina moved to pick up her hat-box, raised one eyebrow and blew him a kiss.

Jock couldn't believe it. 'But you're married to *me*, and this is our *second* date. And I've never even *been* surfing.' She was backing towards the door, shaking her head and laughing.

'Sellie. Sellie, I could fall in love with you,' he said, desperately.

'That makes it a little more tempting,' she allowed, staring at him. 'But, a promise is a promise and a married man is a married man, even if I'm married to him.'

Jock, sitting up now, ran his hands through his hair. 'Selina, we're not married. Captains of ships have no authority to marry people when they're in port. I slipped him $1000 when we shook hands. He must have thought I was trying to get you into bed.'

'Oh, fabulous. Your attitude to money is disgusting. Anyway, he was right, wasn't he?' Selina challenged. 'What am I supposed to do, be grateful for a fling with an eligible shrink? I may be tired, but I'm not a masochist. I'm a little weak at the knees, but I'll get over it. I don't want to be Miss Thursday. I don't even want to be Ms February. So let's just be friends, OK? That way we never have to break up.'

Jock swallowed. 'Maybe we'll never have to break up anyway,' he suggested.

'Who writes this stuff?' said Selina, rolling her eyes.

'Well?'

'You're not *serious*, are you? We've met three times, and you're suggesting a long-term relationship? Look, it's been a long day. A long week. Just . . . settle.'

'OK, so you don't want to be married, you don't want a one-night stand, and you can't see a long-term relationship. What does that leave? Why not just see what develops?'

'What am I, a Polaroid? All right, I'll tell you why not. You won't be able to hack the pace. In five years, at the very outside, you'll be prime-time freak-out crisis material. Thinking back to the days you used to go on dates with the kind of girl who wears lipstick on Sundays. Girls who never argued back. You'll be wondering where the thrill went, and if you're going bald. I don't want to waste my sexual peak on a totally self-centred addled bastard who doesn't know when he's on to a good thing, even if he's had it for a few years. Are you following?'

'Uh, yeah.'

'Good. And because you probably won't even

229

make it to three weeks. You'll flounce into Cantina with the latest thing in designer news readers.'

'Oh,' said Jock, perplexed. 'Anything else?'

'What?'

'Any other things I'm not allowed to do while contemplating a relationship with you?'

'Um, let's see, there's "never sleep with my friends", and "don't blow your nose in the shower".'

'Listen, I'll tell you what, why don't you just stay here tonight. I'll promise not to jump you and we can talk the rest of this stuff out tomorrow.'

'That's better,' smiled Selina. She sat on the edge of the bed, her legs folded under her, and took his hand. He curled around the shape she made, and put his head on her knee. 'Maybe we can just see what develops.'

Jock looked up, with a well-practised, dreamy-eyed, winning smile, and ran an index finger around her left ankle. She felt a frisson that deserved a name all its own, like a newly discovered law of physics. He straightened up, kissed the corner of her mouth, lingered.

'Oh, dear,' she added, and carefully took off his glasses.

'Was that a yes, Ms Plankton?' His voice was soft.

Selina looked at Jock. Jock looked at Selina.

'It depends,' she said. 'Got a condom?'